W9-BDY-354

# The Lash of Señorita Scorpion

**OTHER SAGEBRUSH LARGE PRINT WESTERNS
BY LES SAVAGE JR.**

---

Copper Bluffs

The Legend of Señorita Scorpion
A Circle Ⓥ Western

The Return of Señorita Scorpion
A Circle Ⓥ Western

# The Lash of Señorita Scorpion

## LES SAVAGE, JR.

A Circle Ⓥ Western

# Sagebrush
**Large Print Westerns**

**Library of Congress Cataloging in Publication Data**

Savage, Les.
  The lash of Señorita Scorpion : a western trio/ Les Savage, Jr. —1$^{st}$ ed.
    p.    cm. -- (A Circle V western)
Contents: Trail of the lonely gun — The lash of Señorita Scorpion — The ghost of Jean Lafitte.
  ISBN 1-57490-149-4 (hardcover, alk. paper)
  1. Western stories. 2. Large type books. I. Title. II. Series.
[PS3569.A826L4  1998]
813'.54—dc21                                                  98-27481
                                                                  CIP


Cataloguing in Publication Data is available from
the British Library and the National Library of Australia.

*First Edition*

**Sagebrush Large Print Westerns** are published in the United States and Canada by Thomas T. Beeler, Publisher, Box 659, Hampton Falls, New Hampshire 03844-0659. ISBN 1-57490-149-4

Published in the United Kingdom, Eire, and the Republic of South Africa by Isis Publishing Ltd, 7 Centremead, Osney Mead, Oxford OX2 0ES England. ISBN 0-7531-5797-4

Published in Australia and New Zealand by Australian Large Print Audio & Video Pty Ltd, 17 Mohr Street, Tullamarine, Victoria, 3043, Australia. ISBN 1-86442-255-6

Manufactured in the United States of America by Bookcrafters, Inc.

# ACKNOWLEDGMENTS

"Trail of the Lonely Gun" first appeared in *Action Stories* (Spring, 46). Copyright © 1946 by Fiction House, Inc. Copyright © renewed 1974 by Marian R. Savage. Copyright © 1995 by Marian R. Savage for restored material.

"The Lash of *Señorita* Scorpion" first appeared in somewhat different form under the title "Lash of the Six-Gun Queen" in *Action Stories* (Winter, 47). Copyright © 1947 by Fiction House, Inc. Copyright © renewed 1975 by Marian R. Savage. Copyright © 1998 for restored material by Marian R. Savage.

"The Ghost of Jean Lafitte" first appeared in *Action Stories* (Fall, 45). Copyright © 1945 by Fiction House, Inc. Copyright © renewed 1973 by Marian R. Savage. Copyright © 1997 by Marian R. Savage for restored material.

# CONTENTS

# TRAIL OF THE LONELY GUN

*This short novel first appeared under this same title in* **Action Stories** *(Spring, 46). It was restored, according to the author's original typescript, for its first book appearance in* **The Big Book of Western Action Stories** *(Barricade Books, 1995) edited by Jon Tuska. It is that restored version which was used for the paperback audio edition of "Trail of the Lonely Gun" by Les Savage, Jr., produced by Durkin Hayes, and in what follows. It is perhaps worth noting that the scene of the diamondback rattlesnakes employed during the Hopi snake dance in this story proved an anticipation of the very dramatic use of snakes to be found in Savage's first published novel,* **Treasure of the Brasada** *(Simon & Schuster, 1947), and his ability to create memorable American Indian characters can already be seen here in the mysterious Navajo shaman as well as Abeïto, house chief of Walpi among the Hopi Indians.*

## I

WHEN THE SOUND CAME, JOHNNY VICKERS STIFFENED, and the lever on his sixteen-shot Henry snicked softly to the pull. Moonlight coming in the doorway of the miner's shack fell meagerly across his face, its upper half obliterated by the solid, black shadow laid across it by the brim of his flat-topped hat, his long, unshaven jaw trusting forward in an habitual aggression that drew his lips thin under the aquiline dominance of his nose. The collar of his alkali-whitened denim coat was turned up around the sunburned column of his neck, and his

1

legs were long and saddle-drawn in sweat-stiff Ute leggings with greasy fringe down their seams. Across the gurgle of Granite Creek and on down Thumb Butte Road, he could see Prescott's lights glowing yellow in the soft blackness of the August night.

"Kern?" he said.

"No, Vickers," the man outside answered. "Perry Papago. I'll come in, *sí?*"

The half-breed's figure blotted light from the square gloom of the door momentarily; then he was inside, bending forward slightly, as if to peer at Johnny Vickers. In the shadows, Papago's pock-marked face was barely visible to Vickers, the whites of his eyes pale, shifting enigmas above the mobile intelligence of his broad mouth. He wore nothing but a pair of dirty *chivarras* and a short leather vest, and his shoulders were limned smooth and coppery against the dim glow from outside. Vickers marked the three pounds of Remington .44 still in Papago's holster before he spoke.

"You took a chance walking in like that."

"I didn't know it was so bad," said Papago, and his eyes were taking in the acrid rigidity of Vickers's figure. "But I guess I'd be pretty spooky, too, if I'd been hiding out on a murder charge for over a month. They don't give you much peace, do they, Vickers? I hear Deputy Calavaras almost had you last week up in Skull Valley."

"Never mind," said Vickers.

"Why did you really kill Edgar James, Vickers?" asked Papago. "He was such a nice young man. Just because you and him were rival editors . . . ?"

"He was a swilling rumpot who thought he could find out everything that went on in Arizona Territory by sitting on his hocks in front of that two-bit *Courier*

2

and . . . ." Johnny Vickers stopped, breathing hard, trembling with the effort of holding all the bitterness of this last month in him. Finally he spoke again from between his teeth. "I told you . . . never mind."

"But I will mind," said Perry Papago. "I always liked you, Vickers. If there's one square man with the Indians in Prescott, you're it. Your editorials stopped more than one Indian war from starting. The Moquis at Walpi won't be quick to forget how the Christmas article you wrote kept them from starving in 'Seventy-Four." His voice had lost its former mockery. "We don't blame you for killing James. He bucked every decent thing you tried to do for the Indians. That's why I'm here, Vickers. Any other man, we wouldn't care, but you always played square with us, and we don't want you to get in any bigger fight than you're already in. We don't want you to do this."

Vickers moved faintly, the Henry scraping against his Levi's coat. "Don't want me to do what?"

"I know you're here to meet Judge Kern," said Papago. "Do you know why he wanted you?"

"I know something's happened to his daughter," said Vickers.

"The Apaches got Sherry Kern," said Papago. "The judge wants you to get her back."

The irony of that almost drew a laugh from Vickers. "Why me?" he said finally.

"Because you're his last card," said Papago. "You know those Indians like nobody else does around here, and you're the only one who might be able to reach them without endangering Sherry Kern's life. They took her off the Butterfield stage between here and Tucson, killed the other passengers, burnt the coach. About a week later, Kern was contacted. You know four

3

companies of dragoons were just moved from Tucson up here to Prescott. Kern was given till the end of August to have those troops moved back, or his daughter would be returned to him, dead."

"And Kern thinks it's Apaches?" said Vickers. "What about the Tucson machine? You know how Prescott and Tucson have been fighting for twelve years to see which one becomes the seat of the territorial capital. The legislature's convened in Tucson these past three years, and the Tucson machine's gotten fat on the plum of having it in their town. The movement of these troops to Prescott undoubtedly means the capital's being shifted, too. If the legislature starts convening up here again, the balance of power will shift back to Kern's party, and the Tucson machine will be washed up. You know the machine would do anything to keep that from happening. If they could force those troops back to Tucson, they'd have a big start in keeping the capital there. No legislature's going to meet anywhere in this territory without the protection of the military."

"You're loco," said Papago. "The Tucson machine doesn't have anything to do with this. You know that those dragoons were sent up here by the Department of Arizona as an opening campaign against the northern Apaches. Crook's through with the Tontos, and he's coming up here, that's all. The Apaches just took this way to stop it. Forget the Tucson machine. Forget everything. Just get out of here and don't have anything to do with Kern!"

"I'd rather see the judge first."

"You won't leave?"

"I don't think so."

Papago's hand was stiff, now, and he seemed to incline his short, square torso forward perceptibly.

4

"There are other ways of stopping you besides asking you."

Vickers's big Henry lifted slightly till its bore covered the belt buckle of Navajo silver glittering against Papago's belly. "Go ahead," he said, "if you want to."

"I don't have to," said Papago, and his gaze shifted over Vickers's shoulder. "All right, Combabi, you can take his Henry."

"No, Combabi," said someone else from behind Vickers, "you leave his Henry right where it is."

Vickers stood tense till he heard the movement behind him, then shifted so he could see without taking his gun off Papago. There was no rear door to this old miner's shack, but the roof above the room had caved in, pulling part of the log wall in with it. Combabi must have slipped through the opening while Papago and Vickers were talking; it would have taken a full-blooded Indian to do it without Vickers's hearing. Combabi crouched there now, surprise in the tension of his body, if not in the dark enigma of his hook-nosed face. There was something frustrated about the way he gripped the big Dragoon cap-and-ball in both dirty hands. The man above Combabi on what was left of the decaying log wall had pulled the tails of his pin-striped cutaway up about his lean shanks in order to get there, and a hairy, old beaver hat sat like a stovepipe on his head. The faint glow from the town's lights caught his snowy sideburns and luxurious mustache.

"Kern!" said Vickers. "Looks like we have a potful tonight."

"Getting right spry in my old age," grunted Judge Kern, lowering himself gingerly from the wall with the four-barreled pepperbox still very evident in one slender

5

hand. He waved the ugly little gun at Combabi. "Put away your smoke-box and get on inside."

Combabi moved like a snake, without apparent effort, or sound. He shoved the Dragoon back in its tattered black holster and got to his feet and moved around Vickers sullenly till he stood near Papago, his shifty eyes glittering in the light of the moon filtering into the shack.

"Sorry to be late, Vickers," said Kern, pulling his coat back to stuff the pepperbox in a pocket of his white marseilles waistcoat. "Guess it's just as well, though. I saw this here Indian sneaking in through that hole at the back and decided I'd better see what the arrangements were. He just sat there listening to you talk, so I thought I might as well hear a little of the confabulation, too. Oddly enough, Papago was right about this not being the Tucson machine. I'll admit it fits in with their aims rather fortuitously, but I've had an investigator in Tucson a long time now, and I'd take his word on it. He says, no."

Judge Kern stopped, something coming into his eyes as he stared at Vickers. There was a fierce pride in Kern's high-browed, eagle-beaked face that otherwise held him from any display of emotion. It was probably the only evidence Vickers would ever get of what this meant to the judge. He could sense all the hell the old man must have been through these last days. Then the sympathy was blotted out by the other emotions Vickers had felt toward Kern throughout the preceding weeks. Kern saw it in his face and caught his hard arm.

"I know, Vickers, I know. I've hounded you and hunted you and driven you like an animal this last month, and you don't owe me anything. But you know how close I was to Edgar James. He was like my own

6

son. You couldn't blame a person for wanting the man caught who murdered his own son. You don't know what it took for me to contact you like this, and come to you. But you're my last hope. You're the only man with enough friends among the Indians around here to do any good. We can't make a move with the troops. If we so much as sent a vedette out of town, I'd be afraid the Apaches would kill Sherry. I'm not asking you to do this from the goodness of your heart, Vickers. I'll promise you amnesty, if you get my daughter back. Enough amnesty for you to come back into Prescott and start your paper again, if you want it. Anything, Vickers, anything."

Vickers turned his lean, mordant face down a moment. "Mogollon Kid?" he said finally.

"I don't know who took her," said Kern, desperation leaking into his voice. "I thought you'd know."

"I don't," said Vickers. "I don't even know who the Mogollon Kid is. Nobody does, I guess, any more than they know who bosses the Tucson machine."

Kern grasped his arm. "You will help me, Vickers?"

"No," said Papago, and Vickers whirled toward him, realizing how engrossed they had become in talking. "Vickers won't help you or anybody." Saying that gave Papago the chance to take his jump, knocking aside Vickers's Henry before he could bring it into line, pulling his own Remington at the same time.

Instead of fighting to get the Henry back on Papago, Vickers let it go and threw himself bodily at the man. They met with a fleshy thud, Vickers clutching desperately to turn Papago's gun down as the half-breed cleared leather with it. Behind him, Vickers heard Kern grunt, and thought—Combabi—and then the Remington exploded, jarring Vickers's hand up, the slug hitting

7

earth near enough to Vickers to numb his foot from the impact.

With his free hand, Papago slugged at Vickers's face. Senses reeling to the blow, Vickers stumbled backward and tripped on a body, almost going down. He saw the head of Judge Kern at his feet. Fighting to stay erect, still holding Papago's gun hand with one fist, he caught the half-breed by the belt with his other, swinging the man around. Combabi must have pistol-whipped Kern, for he was just straightening above the judge and his gun was rising toward Vickers. Swung off balance, Papago smashed into Combabi that way. He grunted, and the whole shack rocked as Combabi was knocked back against the wall.

Vickers still had hold of Papago by the belt and gun. Papago gasped with the effort of smashing Vickers in the face again with his free hand, lips peeled away from his white teeth in animal rage. Vickers took that blow, and set himself, and heaved, releasing both his holds on the man.

Combabi was reeling groggily away from the wall, trying to line up his Dragoon again. Papago staggered back into him. They both crashed into the wall and fell to the floor in a tangle of legs and arms. Papago rolled free of Combabi, cursing, and tried to rise. Vickers was already jumping for him, feet first. One moccasin caught Papago in the jaw, knocking his head back against the wall, and again the frame structure shuddered, and dirt showered from the sod roof. Vickers's other foot caught Papago's gun hand, knocking the Remington free. Shouting with pain, Papago tried to rise, but Vickers caught him again in the face with a moccasin. More dirt showered down on them, and Vickers whirled to catch Combabi before the

8

man could rise. The Indian had dropped his cap-and-ball when Papago fell back against him, and Vickers pulled him up by his long, greasy hair and smashed his head against the wall.

"*Pichu-quate!*" shouted Combabi, and his hoarse voice was drowned by the rocking shudder of the building, and then a louder noise. Vickers released the man's hair and jumped backward with earth rattling onto his shoulders.

Just trying to rise from the wall, shaking his head dazedly, Papago was caught in the downpour of sod and timbers as the roof caved in. Vickers saw a rotten beam collapse, one broken end crashing into Papago. Combabi threw himself forward with his eyes shut and his face contorted in fear. They both disappeared in the avalanche of brown earth.

Vickers bent to lift Judge Kern under the armpits and haul him out through the door; then he stopped, realizing the rattling thunder had ceased. Only the far end of the shack had caved in. Kern began groaning and shook his head dully.

"Damned Indian gave me the barrel of that cap-and-ball!"

"Think we ought to pull them out?" queried Vickers.

Kern rose unsteadily to his feet, staring at the pile of earth and timbers at the other end of the room, then glanced at Vickers. His eyes suddenly began to twinkle, and he guffawed. "I guess we better at that, Vickers. Those varmints don't deserve it, but I might lose a night's sleep, if I had it on my conscience, and Papago isn't worth a night's sleep to me."

Combabi's arm was sticking out of the dirt, and he was still conscious when they pulled him free, choking and gasping. Papago took longer to reach, and to revive.

9

Even after he came around, he lay there where they had dragged him outside, breathing faintly, staring up at them with his enigmatic eyes. Slowly, those eyes took on a smoldering opacity and, when he finally rose to his feet, his breathing had become guttural and rasping. Vickers punched the shells from his Remington and handed it back.

Papago glanced at the gun, slipped it back in its holster, and his voice trembled slightly with his effort at control. "You're going after Sherry Kern?"

"What do you think?" asked Vickers.

"You're going after Sherry Kern." It was a statement this time. Papago turned toward his horse, hitched to some mesquite at the site, and Combabi followed him, mounting the roach-backed dun beside Papago's pinto. Papago lifted a leg up, and then, with his foot in the stirrup and one hand gripping his saddle horn, he turned to look at Vickers again, and there was an indefinable menace in his flat, toneless voice. "You're a fool, Vickers. You think you had a lot of men looking for you this last month? It wasn't nothing. It wasn't nothing compared to what you'll be bucking, if you do this. Judge Kern didn't have to swear out any warrant for your arrest. You've signed your own. And it ain't just for your arrest, Vickers. It's your death warrant!"

## II

UP IN THE TORTILLAS THE HEAT STRUCK LIKE THIS IN August, about an hour after sunrise, and there was no breeze to dry the beaded sweat on the hairy, little roan standing there in the coulée where bleeding hearts lay crimson against the black lava. Vickers had rolled himself a cigarette and hunkered down with his back

10

against a boulder so he could see both upslope and down, his Henry in his lap. Three days of riding away from Prescott were behind him, and he had unsaddled the weary bronco completely to rest it. His pale blue eyes took on a gun-metal color in his Indian-dark face, moving deliberately across the slope below him, and his lank, blond hair hung in a sweat-damp cowlick down his gaunt forehead. He gave no sign when the rider came into view. He sat motionless, waiting for the man to rise through the scrubby yuccas down there.

When the rider would have passed him, going on up, Vickers stood without speaking and waited. The man's head turned abruptly, then he necked his big horse around and dropped into the shallow cut Vickers occupied. He stopped the horse and leaned forward in the center-fire rig to peer wide-eyed at Vickers. He was a short, square bulldog of a man with heavy jowls and a mop of russet hair that grew unruly down the middle of his head and receded at his temples above the ears like a pair of pink cauliflowers.

"Vickers?" he said. He descended from the horse with a springy ease to his compact bulk, fishing a cigar from inside his short-skirted, black coat. "Webb Fallon. The Apaches told me you'd be hereabouts this morning. You running in Kern's team, now?"

Vickers took a last puff on his cigarette, studying the cold relentlessness of Fallon's opaque, brown eyes, then dropped the fag and ground it out with a scarred, wooden heel. "Kern said you'd picked up a few things on Sherry."

The name sent something indefinable through Fallon's face, and he didn't speak at once. "I'm glad you're in it," he said finally. "The judge told me he'd try and get you as a last resort. I have found one or two

11

things." He got a leather whang from his pocket. It was worn and greasy, about four inches long. "This, for instance."

"Looks like the fringe off someone's leggings."

"That's right," said Fallon, and let his eyes drop to Vickers's leggings. "Sherry Kern had a handful of them. They came off the leggings of the man who murdered Edgar James."

For a moment, their gazes locked, and Vickers could feel the little muscles twitch tight about his mouth, drawing the skin across his high cheekbones till it gleamed. Meeting his gaze enigmatically, Fallon went on.

"It was one of the pieces of evidence Judge Kern was going to use against you, at the trial. Edgar James must have been close enough to rip it from the murderer's pants. Sherry was the first one to reach Edgar there on Coronado before he died, and he still had this bunch of fringe in his hand. Sherry had kept it in her possession, and, when this turned up, it had some significance for me. As you know, I've been Kern's agent down here for some time, trying to uncover the Tucson machine. One of the Mexicans I've befriended came into Tucson Sunday before last, said a bunch of Apaches with a woman had stopped at his place for food and remounts. They burned his *jacal* and took what horses he had, but he managed to escape into the timber. I went back to his place with him. Found this by the well."

"You think she's trying to leave a trail?" said Vickers.

"It's like her," said Fallon, and that same nameless expression crossed his face as when Vickers had spoken her name before, only more strongly this time. For a moment, Fallon seemed to be looking beyond Vickers.

12

Then, with a visible effort, he brought his eyes back to the man. "You never knew Sherry, did you?"

"Never saw her," said Vickers. "She arrived at Prescott from Austin the night Edgar James was killed."

"You put it nicely."

"Never mind."

"You can admit it to me," said Fallon. "I'm strictly neutral."

Vickers's voice grew thin. "I said . . . never mind."

Fallon's voice held a faint shrug. "All right. So you didn't murder Edgar James. And Sherry Kern came in the night he was killed, and you haven't ever seen her."

"She look anything like the judge?" asked Vickers, feeling the animosity that had descended between them.

"The pride," said Fallon, and again he was looking beyond Vickers with that same thing in his face. Vickers could almost read it now, but could not quite believe it, somehow, in a man like Fallon. "Yes, the pride." Fallon jerked out of it abruptly, waving his hand in frustration at having let Vickers see it. "Black-haired, black-eyed," he said matter-of-factly, "five-six or seven. Big girl. Yes, quite a bit like the judge." He seemed to realize he hadn't used his cigar and bit off the end almost angrily, spitting it out. Then he waved the leather whang. "Think this will do us any good?"

"If she's leaving those for a trail," said Vickers, "it might do us a lot of good."

"Glad you think so," said Fallon. "This was just a lucky strike, and it's left me up against the fence. I don't have your touch with the Indians. That gate's closed to me."

"We'll have to do a sight of riding," said Vickers.

"I imagine," said Fallon.

13

# III

THE PAINTED DESERT EXTENDED THREE HUNDRED miles along the north bank of the Little Colorado, caprices of heat and light and dust changing their hues constantly, a scarlet haze that splashed the horizon, shifting unaccountably into a serried mist of purples and grays from which warmly tinted mesas erupted and knolls of reddish sandstone thrust skyward. Dust-caked and slouching wearily in the saddles of plodding horses, the two men rose from the brackish water of the river toward Hopi Buttes, standing darkly and lonely against the weirdly sunset sky. All afternoon, now, Vickers had been scanning the ground, and finally he found what he had been seeking. He halted his horse, dismounted to study the mound of bluish rocks, topped by a flat piece of sandstone upon which were placed a number of wooden ovals, painted white and tufted with feathers.

Fallon removed the inevitable cigar from his mouth. "What is it?"

"Eagle shrine," muttered Vickers. "The ovals represent eggs. Probably made them during the winter solstice ceremony as prayers for an increase in the eagles. Moquis figure the eagle is the best carrier of prayers to the rain-bringing gods. We should find some boys trapping eagles near here for their annual rain dance."

"You really know, don't you," said Fallon.

Vickers mounted his roan horse. "Where do you think I've been living this last month?"

Fallon moved his animal after Vickers, twisting in the saddle. "Got a funny feeling. Ever get it out here?"

"You mean about being followed?"

Fallon turned sharply toward him. "Then it ain't just a

14

feeling?"

"There was dust on the rim this morning."

"You even got eyes like an Indian," grunted Fallon. "Who do you figure? Apaches?"

"We haven't made a move the Indians don't know about," said Vickers. "It might be them."

"Or someone else?"

"You should know about that," said Vickers.

"How do you mean?" asked the man.

"Doesn't the kidnapping of Sherry Kern by the Indians seem a little too fortuitous, when the Tucson machine would give anything to keep the capital from being moved to Prescott?" asked Vickers.

"It does. But why should I know . . . ?" Suddenly it seemed to strike Fallon, and his face darkened. "I don't like your insinuation, Vickers. I've been working for Judge Kern for a long time."

"And you told him it wasn't the Tucson machine that kidnapped Sherry."

Fallon booted his mare in the flank suddenly, jumping it into Vickers's horse so hard the roan stumbled. Then he grabbed Vickers by the shoulder to pull him around and catch at the front of his Levi's jacket. There was a driving strength in Fallon's fist that held Vickers there momentarily, and the man's wide eyes stared into the eyes of Vickers.

"Listen, I want to get one thing straight, Vickers. I still think you're a murderer, and I don't trust you any more than you trust me. But I'm not going to have you insinuating I have any connection with the Tucson machine. Nobody knows who runs the machine any more than they know who the Mogollon Kid is."

It was Vickers who stopped Fallon. He tore the man's hand off his Levi's jacket and shoved it down toward

15

their waists. Fallon gave one jerk, trying to free his hand, and then stopped, held there more by Vickers's blazing eyes than his grip.

"And I'm tired of being called a murderer, Fallon," said Vickers, through his teeth, "and if you still want to do it, you'd better go for your gun!"

## IV

THE MOQUIS BUILT THEIR EAGLE TRAPS OF WILLOW shoots and deer hide, baiting them with rabbits and concealing themselves inside, waiting to seize the eagles that pounced on the prey, and Vickers and Fallon came across a trap on a flat atop Hopi Buttes. Another man might have been sullen or touchy after a clash like the one Vickers and Fallon had experienced, but Kern's agent sat enigmatically on his mare, watching the Indian youth emerge from the trap, no expression in his wide eyes.

The Moqui boy was lean and drawn as a gaunted bronco, his black hair cut straight across his brow and hanging to his shoulders behind, wearing no more than a buckskin loin cloth and a pair of dirty, beaded moccasins.

"*Buenas días, Señor* Vickers," he said.

"*Buenas días*, Quimiu," said Vickers, answering him in Spanish. "You have grown since I last saw you at Sichomovi."

Quimiu nodded his head in a pleased way without allowing much expression to appear on his face. "You are hunting birds, too?" he asked in Spanish.

"One bird," said Vickers. "A female bird with a black head."

"That is a rare bird," Quimiu told him. "Even more

16

rare if she sheds her plumage in August."

"There was a Hopi down on the Little Colorado who said one of the eagle trappers up here found a feather of that plumage," said Vickers.

Gravely the boy untied a leather whang from his g-string, handing it to Vickers. "You know that I would show it to no other white man."

Vickers passed it to Fallon, and the man compared it with the other whang he had, nodding. "Couldn't miss it. No Apache dyes his leggings like that. First bunch of Ute fringe I've seen in the territory in years." He glanced at Vickers's leggings. "Couldn't miss it."

Vickers drew a thin breath, forcing his eyes to stay on the Indian. "How did the bird fly?"

"Proudly. They must have been riding for days when they passed south of Hopi Buttes, but she still sat straight in the saddle without any fear in her face. Her hair was black as midnight, and long and straight like an Indian maiden's. I saw their dust from here and went down to find out what it was. They didn't see me. There must have been a dozen Apaches"—here the traditional hatred of the Pueblo Indian for the nomad Apaches entered his voice—"and the bird you seek rode behind the leader. She must have fought them, for there were scratches on her face, and her hands were tied, but they had not subdued her."

"Nothing could," said Fallon, and his eyes had that far-away look again, and this time Vickers realized what it was. He had not been able to believe it before, in Fallon. But the same thing was in Quimiu's face now, and Quimiu's description had made the picture of Sherry Kern more vivid in Vickers's mind. That picture had been forming for a long time now, ever since he left Prescott, part of it gleaned from the judge, and other

17

snatches he found on the way to his meeting with Fallon, some from Fallon himself, and now some from Quimiu. Vickers could almost see her, riding proudly and unsubdued in her captivity, her eyes gleaming fiercely, her statuesque body straight and unyielding after a ride that would have exhausted another white woman to the point of collapse. And something else was beginning to form in his mind, or in some other part of him he couldn't name, and it gave him a better comprehension of her capacity to stir other men, or more than stir them. He turned in his saddle to glance at Judge Kern's agent. Yes, even a man like Fallon. Even a cold, passionless man like Fallon.

Then Vickers turned back to Quimiu. "Do you know where they have taken her?"

Quimiu shook his head. "The eagles have some eyries even the Hopi does not know of. There is a Navajo shaman near Cañon Diablo who knows where the birds sleep when the moon rises. I have caught many eagles on his advice."

"Perhaps we had better go there," said Vickers.

"Perhaps you had better not," said a hoarse voice from behind them. "Perhaps you had better stay right here, so I can see what your face looks like when I blow your brains out."

The wind sighing across Hopi Buttes blew cold against the sweat which had broken out on Vickers's brow. His first instinct had been to pull his Henry up from where he held it across his saddle bows. He had stopped his hand from moving with an effort. Finally his rig creaked beneath him as he turned.

Vickers wouldn't have thought a white man could have come up on them like that without giving himself away. This one had. He sat on a rim of the sandstone

18

uplift behind them, a huge, grinning man with a hoary, black beard and a shaggy mane of hair on his hatless head, a ponderous .58 Harper's Ferry percussion pistol in each freckled hand.

"Well, Red-Eye," said Fallon, "you selling whiskey to the Moquis now?"

"I sell it to any man which buys," said Red-Eye Reeves. He wore a pair of moccasins, and his frayed leggings of buckskin were pulled on over red flannels which sufficed for his shirt, the sleeves rolled up to the elbows of his hairy forearms. He waved a Harper's Ferry at Vickers. "The Tucson machine has a price of five hundred on your head. What would you give me not to collect that price?"

It galled Vickers to have to bargain for his life this way, but there was no alternative with those huge percussions in his face. "How much do you want?"

"I didn't say how much. I said what."

"Well."

"You're traveling this country, hunting Sherry Kern," said Red-Eye. "You'll hit a lot of Injun camps. Navajo, Apache, Moqui. I got a load of red-eye that would bring fifty dollars the quart from them redskins. I never been able to reach them before. You're the only one who could take me into Tusuyán and bring me back out again with my scalp still above my beard."

"And after they get through swilling your rotgut, they'll have a war dance and pull a massacre somewhere while they're drunk," said Vickers. "The only reason I could take you into Tusuyán is because the Indians are my friends. You think I'd do that to them?"

Red-Eye Reeves waved one of the Harper's Ferrys again. "This is your alternative, and it's a sort of jumpy one, so you better decide right quick."

19

Vickers took a long breath, speaking finally. "We're heading for a Navajo shaman in Cañon Diablo."

"Suits me," said Red-Eye Reeves. "He'll be good for a gallon at least."

They rode westward from Hopi Buttes, Red-Eye Reeves forking a ratty, little Mexican pack mule and leading a dozen others, *aparejos* piled high with flat, wooden kegs of whiskey. All day Reeves kept pulling at a bottle, and it was evident he had been doing the same before he came on Vickers and Fallon. He reeled tipsily in his saddle, mumbling through his beard sometimes. They were riding through a scrubby motte of juniper east of Cañon Diablo when Vickers drew far enough away for Fallon to speak without being overheard.

"You aren't going through with this?"

"I'll get rid of him as soon as I can," said Vickers.

"Be careful," Fallon told him. "He's drunk most of the time, but he's dangerous. I don't think his real purpose in wanting to come with us is the whiskey."

Vickers glanced at Fallon, pale eyes narrow. "Is he from Tucson?"

"He's been there," said Fallon.

It was the shot, then, cutting off what Vickers had started to say. His roan shied and spooked, starting to buck and squeal, and Vickers threw himself from the horse while he still had enough control over his falling to roll and come up running, the back of his Levi's coat ripped where he had gone through some jumping cholla. "Come back here, you cross-eyed cousin to a ring-tailed varmint!" yelled Red-Eye Reeves from somewhere behind Vickers, and Vickers saw a mule galloping away with wooden kegs spilling in its wake from the dragging *aparejo* pack.

Then they were nearly out of earshot for Vickers,

20

once he threw himself into the monkshood carpeting the ground near the edge of the grove. He lay there in the heady fragrance of the wildflowers, peering toward the mesa ahead of them. The slope was gentle at first, littered with boulders and scrubby timber, then steepened to a veritable cliff, channeled by erosion. Vickers jumped at the movement behind him.

"Never mind," said Fallon, and he crawled in with an old Theur's conversion-model Colt. "It looks like we won't have to worry about getting rid of Red-Eye. He's taking care of that himself."

Still yelling in the distance, Reeves had chased his scattering pack train out into the open beyond them, kicking his scraggly mule after a trio of pack animals that had headed up the slope. He was well onto the rising ground when another shot rang out. His riding mule stumbled, and Reeves went over its head, landing on both feet and running on upslope from the momentum, and both Harper's Ferry guns were in his hands before he stopped.

"Come on out, you misbegotten brother to a spotted hinny and a club-footed jackass. Nobody can treat my babies like that. Nobody can shoot my . . . ."

His own shot cut him off, and Vickers couldn't help exclaiming, because he hadn't seen anybody up there, and he wouldn't have believed anyone could score such a hit with an old percussion pistol.

"I told you he was dangerous," Fallon muttered.

Higher up, a man had risen out of the rocks where he must have been crouched. Both his hands were at his chest, and he stood there a moment, as if suspended. Then he fell forward, rolling out over the sandstone and coming to a stop against some stunted juniper.

Shouting hoarse obscenities, Red-Eye Reeves

21

charged on up the slope. There was something terrible about his giant, black-bearded figure running inexorably upward, and somehow Vickers wasn't surprised to see a man rise farther on up and turn to run. Red-Eye had raised his other Harper's Ferry when the third figure appeared, much nearer, climbing to a rock and holding both hands up, palms toward Reeves.

The drunken whiskey drummer shifted his pistol with a jerk till it bore on that third man. Fallon must have realized it about the same time Vickers did, because he jumped out of the monkshood, shouting: "Reeves, don't, can't you see he . . . ?"

Vickers's shot drowned his voice. The pistol leaped from Reeves's hand, and he yelled in agony, taking a stumbling step forward and pulling the hand in toward him. Fallon turned back to Vickers, his mouth open slightly, and Vickers realized it must have taken a lot for Fallon to show that much emotion.

Reeves was holding out his bloody, shattered hand when they reached him, studying it with a speculative twist to his pursed lips. He looked up and grinned at them. "I didn't think those old Henrys could go that far," he said.

Vickers looked for guile in his face, unwilling to presume the man held no anger at him for shooting the gun from his hand, but he could find none. "Didn't you see that man wanted to surrender?"

"What do I care?" said Red-Eye, bending to pick up his gun and stuffing it in his belt. "The only good Injun's a dead one, to me, and I don't care how my lead catches them, with their hands up, or wrapped around a gun."

Fallon looked at Vickers, then shrugged. "You go and get him. I'll see what we can do for Red-Eye's hand."

22

"The hell with that," growled Red-Eye, wiping his bloody hand against his shirt the way a man would if he had scratched it. "Think one of them damn Henry flatties can do more'n pink a man? It takes one of these babies"—he patted his pistol—"and you'll see what I mean when you find that varmint I pegged higher up. I'm going to get a drink."

He walked off toward where his mules had finally stopped, up on the slope. The Indian who had surrendered was making his way down to them, a gnarled ancient in tattered deerskin, covered with dung and other filth till his stench preceded him a good dozen yards. His watery eyes took some time to focus on them, out of the seamed age of his face, and then he held up a palsied claw of a hand. The single word relegated them to their station, holding neither contempt nor respect.

"*Pahanas*," he said. "White man."

Vickers realized this must be the shaman Quimiu had spoken of. "There was a youth of the *Hopitu-shinumu* named Quimiu in the eagle-trapping ground of Hopi Buttes who told us of a wonder-worker at Cañon Diablo who was in communion with the Trues," said Vickers.

The Trues were the gods of the Pueblos, and, although nothing showed in the shaman's face, there was a subtle change in the tone of his voice. "You must be blessed by the Trues. Quimiu would not have sent white men to me otherwise. I shall then thank you for saving me from the two Apaches who were holding me."

He waved his hand toward the Indian Red-Eye had shot. The second one had disappeared over the lip of the mesa, and, as Vickers moved up to examine the dead one, Reeves came in leading his pack animals. The ball had taken the Indian through the chest, apparently

23

killing him instantly. He wore a pair of Apache war moccasins, made of buckskin, boots really that were hip-length, turned down until they were only knee-high, forming a protection of double thickness against the malignant brush of the southwest. About his flanks was a g-string and a buckskin bag of powder and shot for his big Sharps buffalo gun. Squatting over him, Vickers saw the odd expression catch on Reeves's face.

"Know him?" said Vickers.

Reeves nodded, his drunken humor suddenly gone. "That's Baluno. He rode with the Mogollon Kid."

## V

THE SHAMAN'S *HOGANDA* WAS UP ON THE MESA, overlooking Cañon Diablo which formed the other side, a deep chasm of Kaibab sandstone, yellow at the top and fading into a salmon color as it descended. Vickers had borrowed one of Reeves's mules to round up his spooked roan, and he dismounted from the skittish horse now, loosening the cinch to blow the animal.

"What were those Apaches doing here?" he asked the Navajo.

"Holding me hostage," said the shaman. "They still held enough fear of the shamans not to kill me, but they would not let me leave my *hoganda*."

"But why were they holding you?" asked Vickers. "Is there something they didn't want you to get away and tell?"

"I come up here before the summer Rain Dances for a moon of fasting and praying," said the shaman evasively.

"He'll never tell you anything unless you get him inside that *hoganda*," said Red-Eye, "and you know

24

they won't let a white man in their medicine house."

Vickers held out his hand so the scar showed across his palm. "I am blood brother to Abeïto, the house chief of Walpi."

"You must be the one who saved him from the *pahanas* near Tucson last year," the shaman said enigmatically.

Vickers shrugged, seeing it had done no good, as Abeïto was a Moqui and this man a Navajo. "The white men blamed him for something Apaches did."

Red-Eye put his good hand on the butt of a Harper's Ferry. "We ain't getting nowhere thisaway. Look, you dried-up, old. . . ."

"Never mind, Reeves." Vickers hadn't said it very loud, but it stopped the man. Then Vickers moved closer to the shaman, speaking softly. "I know of *Shi-pa-pu*."

It was the first expression the shaman had allowed to enter his face, and it caught briefly at his mouth and eyes before he suppressed it—awe, or reverence, or fear, Vickers could not tell which. Then, without speaking, he turned and stooped through the low door of the *hoganda*, a conical hut of willow withes and skins, beaten and weathered by the winds of many years on top of this mesa. As Vickers bent to follow, Fallon caught his arm.

"What was it you told him?"

"*Shi-pa-pu*," Vickers murmured. "The Black Lake of Tears, from whence the human race is supposed to have arisen. It's so sacred the Indians rarely say it aloud."

"And no white man is supposed to know about it?"

"I never met another who did," said Vickers. "At least the shaman knows I've been inside their *hogandas* before. That's all we care about."

25

The inside was fetid and oppressive with the same odors the shaman emanated, and Vickers shied away from a *kachina* doll dangling above the door, dressed and beaded and feathered to represent one of the gods. The shaman indicated that they should seat themselves about the flat *Walla pai* basket, woven from Martynia that reposed in the center of the *hoganda*. Then the medicine man seated himself and stirred the coals of the fire before the empty basket until they glowed, lighting a *weer* he produced from a buckskin bag at his belt. This sacred cigarette he passed around, and, while each of them puffed on it, he began murmuring incantations over the dying light of the coals. It was almost pitch black inside the hut when the buckskin thong appeared, and Vickers couldn't have sworn how it got there. The shaman continued muttering, three feet away from the basket, but Fallon drew in a hissing breath, reaching toward the piece of rawhide fringe now residing in the bottom of the flat basket. Vickers caught his hand, pulling it back.

"Quimiu had such an object also," said Vickers. "A feather, he said, dropped from a black-headed bird who shed her plumage in August."

"A goddess, rather," murmured the shaman, and Vickers could feel something draw him up, because he sensed it coming again, and his breathing became audible, and swifter, "a goddess sent by the Trues to prove to the Apaches what coyotes they are. Nothing they had done could subdue her. Their leader himself wished her favor, but she bit his hand when he tried to touch her. Even the dust and sun and weariness of the long ride could not hide her beauty. Her eyes were not as black as her hair, and once, when she turned fully to me, it was as if I had stared into the swimming smoke of

26

a campfire, and another time, when she looked at the leader of the Apaches, it was as if I had seen lightning. Other of the Dineh', like Quimiu, have seen her, and, as long as the sacred *weer* is smoked in the *hoganda*, it will be told how the goddess rode through our land, leaving signs to the favored ones."

From the corner of his eye, Vickers could see Fallon bending forward that same way, his mouth parted slightly, his wide eyes rapt. Suddenly he seemed to feel Vickers's gaze on him, and closed his mouth, leaning back, glancing almost angrily at Vickers.

"How did you get the sign?" said Vickers, motioning toward the buckskin whang in the basket.

"The Apaches were apparently expecting to find water in the Red Lake, but it had been dry for a moon, and there was none. They would not have revealed their passing to me unless they were desperate for water. They forced me to show them my sacred sink on the mesa, where the sun cannot reach the water which the Rain Gods have brought and dry it up. Then they left the one named Baluno and his companion to guard me and keep me from telling of them until they were safely away."

Fallon's eyes were on Vickers now, in a covert speculation, as he spoke: "The Mogollon Kid?"

The shaman sat, staring into the basket without answering Fallon. The fire had died completely now, and the light from the smoke hole was rapidly fading as night fell outside, enveloping the interior of the *hoganda* in darkness. Vickers could barely see Red-Eye Reeves across the basket. He saw the man glance at him now, and there was that same speculation as Vickers had seen in Fallon's face. Vickers felt his hands tighten around the Henry across his knees. In a few moments it

27

would be so intensely dark that none of them could see the others.

"I thought the shaman feared none but the Trues," said Vickers, and his body was stiffening for the shift.

The shaman's voice came abruptly from the gloom, almost angrily. "How do I know if it was the Mogollon Kid?"

"I have heard the Indians feared the Mogollon Kid as much as their own gods," said Vickers. "He must have the power of the Trues, if he can shut a shaman's mouth." Even that failed to elicit any response from the shaman. "If you can't tell us who it was," said Vickers, "perhaps you can tell us where they are bound."

Vickers had seen the incredible legerdemain of these wonder workers. Once he had seen a shaman make corn grow in the bare dirt floor of a *hoganda*, and it had convinced and amazed even his Occidental realism. But this came so unexpectedly that it held him spellbound as it occurred. A faint blue glow descended from the smoke hole of the hive-like structure, until their four figures were bathed in an eerie light, faces drawn and taut with a sudden tension. The piece of buckskin fringe was revealed momentarily in the basket, shifting like a small snake with a life of its own till it pointed due north. Then the light was extinguished abruptly.

In the following blackness Vickers recovered enough from the sight to do what he had planned. Still sitting in the cross-legged position they had all assumed, he placed his hands on either side of him and shifted himself about twelve inches to the right with his legs yet crossed, speaking as he did to mask any sound.

"The sacred sign points to Tusuyán."

"Yes," said the shaman. "The Dance of the Snake is being held at Walpi this year . . . ."

The shot thundered, rocking the *hoganda*, deafening Vickers. He sat rigid with his back against the willow frame of the hut, his Henry cocked across his lap, waiting for whoever came for him. There was a shout, a muffled struggle in the utter darkness, then the *hoganda* shook violently. Outside, the animals had been spooked by the shot, whinnying and nickering and shaking the ground as they tore up their picket pins and galloped back and forth before the door. Vickers knew what a target anybody would be going out that door, and he sat there till silence had fallen again. Finally the spark from a flint and steel caught across the hut. He jerked his Henry that way. It was the shaman, throwing fresh juniper shavings on the dead coals. He lit the fire and shuffled across the room to where Vickers had risen. There was no one else in the *hoganda*.

The shaman fingered the bullet hole in the hide wall. "It would have killed you if you'd been sitting one *paso* to the left," he muttered. "I wonder why they wanted you dead?"

Vickers turned toward the door. "I don't wonder why, so much, as which one."

## VI

FOR CENTURIES THE REGION IN NORTHEASTERN Arizona Territory had been known as the province of Tusuyán, and the Pueblos living there as Moquis, or Hopis, from their own name for themselves, *Hopitu-shinumu*. Walpi was one of these pueblos, perched atop a somberous mesa, a giant block of sandstone reaching up from the flatlands about it, the tiered mud houses on its top barely visible from below. It was August of the second year, and groups of Indians from the other

29

pueblos and from the Navajo camps to the east had been passing up the trail to Walpi all day, raising nervous flurries of gray dust over the fields of corn and squash near the village.

Knowing it would be suicide to go out the door of the shaman's hogan there above Cañon Diablo, if anyone was outside, Vickers had unlashed some of the deer hides at the back, crawling out that way, only to find that both Red-Eye Reeves and Fallon were gone, with all the animals, including his roan.

He had trailed them on foot, but, being mounted, they soon outdistanced him. He could read sign of someone on the roan driving Red-Eye's mules, but could find no other horse prints, and concluded Fallon had not left the *hoganda* with Red-Eye.

A week after Cañon Diablo, Vickers was plodding up the trail toward Walpi behind a party of Apaches on wiry little mustangs. Ordinarily the Apaches and Navajos were enemies of the Pueblos, but, during the Snake Dance, hostilities were suspended, and other tribes were allowed to view the ceremonies. The houses atop the mesa were built three stories high, each story set back the length of one room on the roof of the lower level, forming three huge steps, with rickety ladders reaching each roof from the one below. What passed for the streets and courtyards in front of the houses were filled with a milling crowd of Indians, Moqui women in hand woven *mantas* holding dirty brown babies to their breasts, tall, arrogant Navajo men with their heavy silver belts and turquoise bracelets, a few shifty Apaches like strange dogs, standing apart in their little groups and bristling whenever they were approached, turkey-red bandannas on their greasy black hair, perhaps a Sharps hugged close.

30

Stopping near the entrance from the trail to the mesa top, Vickers was aware of their suspicious eyes on him, and an ineffable sensation of something not quite right filled him. Then a Navajo stumbled through the crowd toward Vickers, pawing at a big Bowie in his silver belt, and Vickers knew what it was.

"*Pahanas*," growled the Navajo, shoving a Moqui woman roughly aside, and Vickers could see how bloodshot his eyes were. A pair of Moqui braves moved in from where they had been standing beneath an adobe wall, and they were drunk, too. As Vickers opened the lever on his Henry, he saw the Mexican rat-mule standing in a yonder courtyard, its *aparejo* pack ripped off and laying at the animal's feet, empty kegs strewn all about the hard-packed ground.

"*Pahanas, pahanas!*" It was a shout, now, coming from a bibulous Apache, running in from the other side. Vickers had waited till the last moment, but, just as he was about to raise his Henry up to cover them, someone else shouted from the rooftop of a nearby building.

"No, not *pahanas. Hopitu-shinumu.* He is my blood brother."

It was Abeïto, house chief of Walpi, swinging onto one of the rawhide-bound ladders and climbing down with a quick, cat-like agility. He was a small, compact man in white doeskin for the coming ceremony, a band of red Durango silk about his black, bobbed hair. The Moquis stopped coming at Vickers, and the Navajo moved grudgingly aside, still clutching his knife, to let the house chief through. Vickers embraced Abeïto ceremoniously, as befitted a blood brother, but he saw it in the house chief's eyes as Abeïto pulled him through the milling crowd toward his own dwelling.

"Reeves is here?" he said to Abeïto. "Why did you let

31

him sell that whiskey to your people, brother? You could have stopped it."

"He didn't sell it," said the house chief, pulling him urgently toward the ladder.

"But he must have," said Vickers, trying to understand the evasive darkness in Abeïto's eyes. "The *Moquenos* never took things without paying. They are not Apaches. What's happening here, Abeïto? You're still house chief, aren't you?"

"Yes, yes," said the Moqui. "We can't talk here, brother."

Abeïto glanced nervously at a group of Apaches standing near the ladder. One of them, with a Colt stuck naked through a cartridge belt about his lean middle, had a keg of whiskey. They were watching Vickers, shifting back and forth restlessly, talking in sullen tones, and Vickers caught the name as he reached for the ladder, and stopped.

"Is that it?" he asked Abeïto.

"Please, don't stop out here. Is what it?"

"You heard what they said."

"Brother, for your own good. . . ."

"Are you afraid of him, too?" Vickers asked. "There was a youth at Hopi Buttes too afraid even to speak his name, and a shaman at Cañon Diablo. If the shamans are afraid of him . . . ."

"I am house chief of Walpi," said Abeïto, drawing himself up, "head of the Bear Clan. Never did I expect to hear such an insult from my blood brother."

"Then is that it?"

Abeïto hesitated, glancing about him, face dark. "The Mogollon Kid?" he said, finally.

Vickers clutched at his coat. "Is he here? The Kid. Who is he, Abeïto?"

32

"I did not say he was here," said the Moqui, grabbing Vickers's elbow. "Brother, if you value your life, get up that ladder into my house. We can't talk out here. Only their respect for my position holds them now. They have known of your coming for days. I sent a runner out to turn you back, but he must have missed you. Please . . ."

The spruce ladder popped and swayed beneath Vickers's weight. On the first terrace an eagle was fluttering in an *amole* cage, one of the birds trapped at Hopi Buttes and brought here for the rain ceremonies, to be killed after the last *kachinas* came in July, the Indians believing the eagle's spirit would carry prayers for rain to the Trues. Abeïto shoved aside the heavy *bayeta* blanket hanging over the doorway leading into the rooms on the second level, allowing Vickers to go in first. A squaw was sitting on the floor inside before the cooking stone the *Moquenos* called a *tooma*, mixing blue corn meal with water to form a thin batter for *pikama*. Vickers spoke their language to some extent, but, when she looked up and saw him, she said something so fast he couldn't catch it.

"He is my blood brother," the house chief told her. She said something else, rising from the *tooma*. Abeïto took an angry breath and motioned toward the door. "Get out," he told her. "Get out."

When she was gone, he turned to Vickers. "You see how it is? You can't stay here. I am violating all the laws of hospitality now, but it is for your own good, brother. For weeks we have heard of your search for the black-haired woman. I knew you, and I knew sooner or later you would arrive here. She is not here, believe me."

"Then who is?" said Vickers. "What's happening?

33

Why have you so little control over your people? Surely it was not your wish that they took Reeves's fire-water. You know what will happen with everyone drunk like this. You have a hard enough time maintaining peace among your people and the Navajos and Apaches as it is. Why were they talking of the Mogollon Kid? Where is he?"

A man shoved aside the *bayeta* blanket in the doorway, stepping inside. "Here he is," he said.

Vickers had lived and traveled among the Indians long enough to acquire some facility at hiding his emotions when it was necessary, but he felt his mouth open slightly as he stared past Abeïto's white doeskin shoulder at the man swaggering in the doorway, one hand holding aside the curtain to reveal the Apaches behind him, the other hand hooked in his heavy cartridge belt near enough to the big, blued Remington .44 he packed. His lean, avaricious face was scarred deeply from smallpox, and the whites of his eyes were pale, shifting enigmas above the thin, mobile intelligence of his broad, thin-lipped mouth.

"Perry Papago," said Vickers emptily.

Papago grinned without much mirth, moving on in, and Combabi followed him on silent, bare feet, shifting black eyes unwilling to meet Vickers's gaze, and the other Apaches blotted out the light from the door behind, the bores of their Sharps rifles covering Vickers.

"This is why your blood brother has so little control over his people, Vickers," said Papago, tapping the short, buckskin vest covering his bare chest. "I've taken over. It's for their own good. Four troops of dragoons in Prescott and more coming up as soon as the Department of Arizona can shift them. If the Indians don't organize now, they'll be wiped out. The Navajos and Apaches

34

are all ready. All we need are the Moquis, and we'll have them as soon as the Snake Dances are over. I tried to talk some sense with Abeïto, but he wouldn't listen. Get his people drunk enough and they'll listen. There are half a thousand warriors in the seven pueblos of Tusuyán, Vickers. What do you think your bluecoats can do when I add them to my Apaches?"

Vickers was bent forward, his voice intense. "You've got the girl?"

Papago's eyes raised slightly. "Girl?"

"You know, Papago. You're the Mogollon Kid? You've brought her here to this. We found your man, Baluno, at Cañon Diablo." Vickers was trembling. "Don't try and deny it, Papago. What have you done with her? What have you done with Sherry Kern?"

Papago pursed his lips, and something mocking entered his voice. "I didn't know you felt that way about her, Vickers. She must be a beautiful woman."

"Papago . . . ."

"Brother!" Abeïto caught Vickers as he lunged forward at Papago. Then he turned to the half-breed. "Let him go, Papago. He has always been our friend. Even your friend. Take me in his place. Whatever you were going to do with him, do with me."

"No," said Papago, and lifted his hand off his cartridge belt to motion at his men, and they began slipping in and moving around behind Papago and Combabi, dark, menacing Apaches, the whites of their eyes shining in the semi-gloom. "No, Abeïto. I tried to stop Vickers from this at the beginning, but he wouldn't listen. As you say, he has been our friend, and I didn't want him mixed up in it. But now, he has come too far. Take him!"

This last he called to his men, and there was the

35

abrupt scuffle of feet across the hard-packed floor. Vickers tore loose of Abeïto, trying to bring his Henry into line and snap down the lever all in one action. He saw Combabi go for his cap-and-ball, whirled that way, already seeing he would be too late, because the Indian's Dragoon was free even before Vickers heard the metallic click of his cocked Henry. Then a white figure hurtled in front of Vickers, and the thunder of Combabi's shot filled the small room. Vickers pulled his gun up in a jerky, frustrated way, till it was pointing at where Combabi had been, hidden now by the other man. Stunned, Vickers watched the man in white doeskin sink to the floor in front of him, and Combabi was visible again, his cap-and-ball dirtying the soft gloom with a wreath of acrid, black powder smoke. Perry Papago stood to the other side, and he was looking at Abeïto, sprawled on the floor. Then he lifted his eyes.

"You better drop it, Vickers. My Apaches got their Sharps rifles loaded now. You haven't got a chance."

All around him, Vickers was aware of the Indians, standing with their muzzle loaders trained on him. He dropped the Henry, butt plate striking first, then the long barrel, and went to his knees beside Abeïto. It was then he became aware of the hubbub outside. The *bayeta* blanket was torn aside, and a Moqui brave thrust into the room, followed by a pair of *principales*, white-headed dignitaries of Walpi's governing body. They stopped when they saw Abeïto, and other Moquis, crowding in from behind, stumbled against the *principales*. Lifting his head toward them, Vickers did not know what he was going to say, when he saw the gun in Papago's hand. It was Combabi's cap-and-ball, still reeking of the black powder.

36

"*Pahanas*," said Papago, waving his hand toward Vickers, then holding the gun up. "Your house chief found the *pahanas* with one of your women."

"No!" Vickers was surprised to hear Abeïto's voice. He lifted the man's head higher, and Abeïto shuddered in his arms, trying to get the words out. "He cannot . . . my blood brother cannot . . . have done that," said the house chief incoherently. "The Trues sent him. He is the only one whoever befriended us. The Trues sent him."

Abeïto sighed deeply, and his body was a sudden weight in Vickers's arms. Then the fetid smell of sweat and buckskin gagged Vickers, and rough arms were pulling him off Abeïto. He was still staring at the dead house chief, a thin pain somewhere inside him now. They had known a lot together. It was odd he should remember that time he had caught his hand between the bed and the platen of his first press. He had wanted to cry then.

"You wanted to see the girl?" It was Papago's voice, entering Vickers's consciousness. "You'll see her now, Vickers. You thought it was the Tucson machine? That's funny. I'm sorry it had to be this way, but you were on the wrong horse from the beginning, I guess, even about the machine. We tried to stop you, didn't we? Other men had been sent out to find her, and I didn't go out of my way to stop them. I stopped them, but I didn't go out of my way to do it. I wouldn't have ridden from here to Prescott to stop them the way I did you. But I knew what a mistake it would be to let you get started, Vickers. I'd already gotten here with Sherry when I got word Kern had contacted you to meet him there in that miner's shack outside Prescott. You almost made it anyway, didn't you? You came farther than anyone else ever did. You're the only living white man

37

who knows I'm the Mogollon Kid."

They were hauling him roughly past Papago and the other Apaches. The strange, dazed emotion of seeing Abeïto dead had held it back, but now the full comprehension of what had happened struck Vickers, filling him with the first impulse to struggle since Papago had told the Apaches to get him. Vickers threw his weight against the *Moquenos*, managing to halt them momentarily, and turned enough to see Papago's Indian ally.

"Combabi," he said, and perhaps it was the utter lack of any vehemence, or emotion in his voice which made the Indian's face pale slightly. "I'll kill you for that."

Somewhere outside, the big medicine drums they called the *tombes* had begun to beat. Vickers knew what that meant. The Snake and Antelope fraternities had conducted their secret rites in the *estufas* for eight days, fasting and purifying themselves, and now the *tombes* were heralding their readiness for the public dance.

## VII

THE FLOOR WAS HARD AND ROUGH BENEATH VICKERS as he sat up. They had taken him to the eastern end of the mesa and thrown him into one of the ceremonial *kivas*, a room dug out of the solid rock and roofed over about a foot above the level of the ground, a ladder leading down into it from above. There was an air hole in the roof. His eyes had been accustoming themselves to the semi-gloom when he realized there was someone else in here. At first, it was only a dim, unrecognizable figure, standing against the wall on the far side. Then he saw it was a woman and realized she had been standing there like that, watching him, ever since he had come in.

38

And finally, he recognized her.

It was like a physical blow. He felt his breath coming out audibly between parted lips. He had tried to prepare himself for it, all the way from his first knowledge of her, telling himself preconceived notions were always wrong. Yet no preconceived idea he had formed could match this, now. They had given her a split Crow skirt of buckskin to enable her to ride, and it only seemed to delineate the tall, statuesque lines of her body. What had Fallon said? The pride? Her white linen blouse had been smudged by dirt and torn by chaparral, but it still shone pale in the dusky light.

"Who are you?" she asked. "Why do you stare at me like that?"

He had no right to let it catch him like this, with the grief of knowing Abeïto was gone still so fresh in his mind. Yet he could not help it, and he knew, somehow, that Abeïto wouldn't mind. He was still gazing at her, hardly conscious of his actions as he fished the three whangs of fringe from his pocket.

"I had a handful of them," said the woman, seeing what he held. "Several people know that I possess them. I tried to leave a trail. I thought, if they found them, somehow they could follow me." She motioned with her hand. "You . . . ?"

"It began to be like I was following someone I'd known all my life," he said. Then he was leaning toward her, still on his knees, something urgent crossing his lean face. "It can happen, can't it? I mean, without ever having seen you, it can happen, to a man, that way?"

Her bosom moved faintly beneath the soiled blouse, and her eyes were still held to his. "What can happen? What way?"

"I wouldn't have believed it could happen," he said,

39

getting to his feet. "Not without knowing you. Not without even seeing you. I tried to tell myself I was a fool. At night I'd lie there in my blankets and think about it and laugh at myself, or try to. I couldn't really laugh, because it was happening, whether I believed it or not."

Suddenly, there seemed to be an affinity between them. Perhaps it was the way they were gazing at each other, perhaps something less physical than that. Vickers saw a growing comprehension in the woman's eyes, and she bent forward slightly, searching for something in his face, her voice barely audible, as if she feared to break a spell.

"Believe what? What was happening?"

"It started so long ago," he said. "Do you think I'm crazy? In Prescott, I guess, when the judge told me . . . ."

"My father?"

He had hardly heard her. "I'd known of you, of course, but only vaguely. The judge didn't tell me much. Just what you meant to him. Not even a description. But it must have started, even then. Later, it was more than that. Do you think I'm crazy? A man named Fallon. He told me some. Your pride? It was like getting a glimpse of you through a window. Not much. Not enough, but enough to want more. Then an Indian boy. He told me the way you rode. About your hair. It was the way he told me. They have a sensitivity to something like that no one else possesses. Just at that age. You know?"

She must have understood what he was trying to say, now. She wanted to smile, and couldn't. Staring at him, her eyes were soft and smoky, and her brows were drawn together in a strange, intense way, as if she were

40

groping to define some emotion within herself.

"I know," she conceded, at last, almost whispering.

"After that, a shaman," said Vickers. "An old man. Too old for anything like the boy. And yet, even him. Telling me about your eyes. And after I left him, I wasn't even trying to laugh at myself any more. It can happen, can't it, that way? Do you think I'm crazy?"

She was still gazing at him, lost in it, like a child enraptured by a storyteller, and she moistened her lips, speaking almost dreamily. "No," she said, and drew a quick, soft little breath, as if faintly surprised at her own words, "no, I don't think you're crazy."

"Well," said a rough voice from the dark corner, "now that you've told the fair maiden of your undying love, maybe you'd better let her know who you are."

Both the girl and Vickers stiffened, as if snapped from a trance. Then Vickers turned to see the big, bearded man in the long-sleeved, red flannels sitting cross-legged against the far wall.

"Reeves," said Vickers stupidly.

"Yeah, little old Red-Eye himself," said Reeves. "I guess I should have waited for you to come with me and help sell that rotgut, shouldn't I? Those damn' Apaches took my goods and dumped me in their calaboose. What was all that shooting in the shaman's diggings at Diablo?"

"I think you know," said Vickers.

"Do I?" said Reeves slyly. "What happened to Fallon?"

"He ran out the same way you did."

When Reeves had first spoken, the woman had turned toward the bearded man. Now she was looking at Vickers again. "Mister Reeves said you were going to introduce yourself."

41

"I'll do the honors," grinned Reeves. "Johnny, this is Miss Sherry Kern. Miss Kern, meet Johnny Vickers."

All the blood seemed to drain from her face at that instant.

"Johnny Vickers!" she said, and there was a loathing in her voice. "Johnny Vickers," and she spat it out the second time, pulling a handful of fringe from the pocket of her shirt, holding it out in front of her for him to see. "I was at the Butterfield station on Union Street when I heard the shot. It was just around the corner, right in front of the *Courier*. I was the first to reach him, and he was still alive. 'Get to Johnny Vickers,' he said, and this was in his hand . . . ." Her fingers closed on the handful of fringe spasmodically and then opened as she flung it at Vickers, taking a step backward, her mouth twisting as she wiped her hand down her skirt. "'Get to Johnny Vickers' he said, and then he died!"

Vickers held out his hand, something chilling him suddenly. "You think . . . ?"

"You know what I think," she said, the words torn from her in a hollow, bitter way. "Why do you suppose I'd come to Prescott that evening? Edgar James and I were going to be married the next day!"

## VIII

THE DARKNESS TREMBLED TO THE INCESSANT RHYTHM of the *tombes* now, and beneath the hollow, muffled beat, the other sounds had begun, as the *Moquenos* and Navajos and Apaches gathered toward the end of the mesa for the dance. Vickers hunkered in bitter silence against the wall opposite Red-Eye Reeves, looking neither at the bearded man nor at Sherry Kern.

Sure there were hunks missing out of his fringed

42

leggings. Every man who wore leggings cut the fringe off at some time or another when he was without any other kind of lashings to repair his saddle or tie his duffel or a thousand other things they could be used for. So there were hunks cut out of the fringe on his pants. And no other man wore Ute leggings around here. All right. So the Utes dyed their fringe differently. All right. And so Edgar James had told her to get Johnny Vickers. The hell with it! He shifted angrily, running his tongue across dry, cracked lips. That was what he'd come for. He should have known it from the beginning. Not the way a Moqui boy looked when he described her, or the way Fallon lost himself when he talked of her. Not any of that. This!

Vickers wanted to spit and didn't have enough saliva in his mouth to do it. His head raised abruptly to the scraping noise from the direction of Reeves. The bearded man had stiffened and risen to his feet, turning to face the wall, backing off toward the center of the room. The walls were curtained with red *chimayo* blankets, and one of these was thrust aside. The room being sunk into the earth this way, it had never entered Vickers's head that the blankets might conceal a doorway. The portal that opened behind a blanket was a heavy oak piece, set in the solid rock, and a man stood there with one hand holding the *chimayo* blanket back. His face was painted black to the mouth, and from there down to the neck, white. The rest of his body, naked to the waist, was a lake-red. About his square belly was a dancing skirt of wool, with fox skins dangling behind, rattles tied to his naked ankles.

"Your fate has been decided, Vickers," he said in English. "It seems Abeïto tried to tell them you were sent by the Trues before he died. Otherwise they would

43

have killed you outright. As it is, the *principales* have been debating, and their decision is that, if you were really sent by the gods, you can survive the Snake Dance."

Vickers was on his feet, staring at the man, and it had struck him by now. "Fallon," he said. "Webb Fallon."

Fallon shut the door quickly behind him, coming forward to be surrounded by the three of them, forgetting their hatred and bitterness in this moment enough to come together. Fallon caught at Vickers's arm.

"Not much time for explanation now. I got away from Diablo on your roan. Came across one of these Antelope men out getting rattlesnakes for the dance. Knocked him on the head and took his outfit. That Navajo shaman said the Snake Dances were being held at Walpi, and the buckskin thong in the basket was pointing north. I took the chance that implied Sherry had been taken here. Climbed the cliff on this south side during the night, hunted till daylight for her without success. In this monkey suit, I could move around the pueblo pretty free as long as it was dark. Had to hide in one of their *estufas* during the day. I don't speak their language. But neither do the Apaches. Some *Moqueno* was talking to an Apache in Spanish outside the *estufa*. The court where they're going to hold the dance is on a lower level than the upper part of the mesa. Guess you know this. It's where this door leads. It's how we'll escape."

"But it's a sheer cliff on the south side of the court," said Vickers. "We'll have to go through the whole pueblo to get out."

"I don't mean that way," said Fallon. "They'll let you all go, if you survive the Snake Dance."

"That's impossible," snapped Vickers. "There's over

44

a hundred rattlers in the ceremony. A white man wouldn't last a minute in that court."

"It's the only way. You can't fight your way through a thousand drunk Indians without even a pocketknife in your hands." Fallon turned toward the door. A *tombe* had begun thumping out there. He spoke swiftly. "They're starting. This has to be fast. When I heard what the *principales* had decided and knew you were in here, I managed to get inside that cottonwood booth where they keep the snakes in a big buckskin bag. I let one out, stepped on its tail before it could coil, closed the bag on the others. Then I grabbed it behind the head and extracted the fangs. Did the same with four others. Sweat made this paint on my body wet enough to daub a circle of it around the tail of each snake. You can't miss it. Whatever they make you do with those snakes, pick the ones with the paint on them."

"But there'll be others," said Vickers. "They have a dozen at a time crawling around that court."

"I'll see that they don't bite you," said Fallon.

The girl's face darkened. "What do you mean?"

Fallon left without answering her. Vickers could feel sweat dampening his face as he stood there with the girl and Red-Eye. The fight going on inside Sherry was evident to him in her rigid body, her set face. He didn't blame her. He felt a fear growing in himself. There was something ghastly about the thought of that courtyard out there full of writhing, hissing snakes. Vickers reached out and touched her impulsively, and then let his hand slide off as she turned toward him. He didn't know whether the look on her face was for him or for the snakes.

The door was thrust open, and a pair of braves in the same costume as Fallon had worn entered, carrying the

45

sacred rattles known as *guajes*. The design on their kilts indicated they were of the Bear Clan, and one of them told Vickers in sonorous tones of the sentence imposed on them by the *principales*, then nodded his head toward the door.

Vickers took a deep breath and stepped out, followed by Sherry. An audible sighing sound went up from the crowds lining the tops of the houses on the west of the courtyard, and then a shout, as the Apaches saw the girl following Vickers. There was no ladder from the housetops into the courtyard, but Perry Papago dropped off the first roof, landing like a cat, running out to the captain of the Antelope Society where he stood with his dancers by the sacred cottonwood booth called the *kee-si*.

"There is no reason for the girl to be tested," he told the Moqui, and Vickers realized Papago feared her death would leave him with no hold over the troops in Prescott. "*Pahanas* Vickers is the only one on trial."

"They are all *pahanas*," said the captain. "If they are sent by the Trues, they must prove it. This is the judgment of the *principales*."

"No," shouted Papago. "Combabi, Assaya, Jerome . . . ."

At his call, his Apaches began surging toward the edge of the roof, pushing through the other Indians. Combabi dropped off a house into the court, pulling his cap-and-ball. Then he stopped, with the gun held there in both hands. At the signal of the captain's hand, one of the Antelope men had swung aside the curtain of the *kee-si* and reached in to unlace the top of one of the buckskin bags holding the snakes, and the first rattler slid out, hissing and writhing. Instinctively, Papago jumped back against the wall, and another big, ugly

46

diamondback rattler slithered from the *kee-si*. Combabi backed up, a twisted revulsion on his face. Perhaps it was the very primitive horror of the slimy death in these creatures that held him from firing, or perhaps that he knew how sacred the snakes were to the *Moquenos*, and how the whole pueblo would mob him, if he dared shoot.

Behind him, Vickers heard a strangled sound. At first he thought is was Sherry, and looked toward her. But she was standing rigidly beside him, a white line about her tightly shut lips, staring wide-eyed at the half-dozen huge snakes writhing across the floor of the courtyard. It was Reeves.

"Vickers," he said hoarsely, "they ain't gonna make us dance with them snakes. Not white men. Not rattlers like that."

It surprised Vickers. He hadn't expected it from Reeves, somehow. He remembered how Reeves had gone out to get those Apaches at Cañon Diablo, and how he had reacted to the gunshot wound.

"You heard Fallon," said Vickers. "He's fixed some of the snakes. It's our only way."

"No." Reeves's palms were spread out against the rock on either side of him as the Antelope man let out another hissing snake. "No, Vickers, you're the only one on trial. Papago's right, you're the only one on trial. Ain't no reason the rest of us have to dance with those snakes. I don't see any with paint daubed on their tails. They're real, Vickers. I seen a man bit by one of them diamondbacks last year. He swelled up like a balloon." Sweat was streaking the grime in Reeves's face now, leaking down into his beard. "Tell them I don't have to do it, Vickers. Make up some excuse. You can. You know them. Tell them I got a special chit from these

47

Trues, or whatever they are. I just come along. Tell them, Vickers . . . ."

The girl was still standing there like that, and a faint line of red showed across her chin, and Vickers could see now how her teeth were clamped into her bottom lip, and the sight of Reeves disgusted him suddenly. He grabbed the man's arm.

"Come on. You'll spoil it all. If we were sent by the Trues, we wouldn't act like this. They'll get suspicious, and it'll be all over. You've got to trust Fallon."

"No!" Reeves tore from Vickers's grasp, a glazed look in his eyes, and fell back toward the rock wall. "Please, Vickers, get me out of this. I'll do anything else. Man or devil. I've fought 'em all in my time. Injun or white, black or yellow, man or beast. I fought a grizzly once. See? See the scar on my chin? But not this, Vickers. You can't just walk in there and start playing with them diamondbacks. They'll have you bloated like a *cimarrón* carcass in five minutes. Please, Vickers. Anything. I'll do anything. Tell them, Vickers . . . !"

"Shut up!" Vickers slapped him across the face, knocking his head back against the wall. The Indians were watching them now. "If you spoil our only chance here, I'll kill you myself. Now get up like a man and take it. I thought you were a man. Down at Cañon Diablo I thought I hadn't ever seen that kind of nerve before."

"This ain't the same." Reeves was huddled back against the wall, his lower lip slack and wet. "Snakes, Vickers, snakes. It ain't the same. There's something special about them. Anything else, Vickers. I told you. Anything else. Not snakes, Vickers. I seen a man bit. Anything but snakes. I didn't come for this!"

48

"What did you come for then?" Vickers had both hands buried in his shirt, shaking him savagely. "What did you come for?"

"To get the gal. You know that. Get me out, and I'll tell you. Get me out. I'll do anything, Vickers."

Vickers shook him again. "It was you took the shot at me back in the shaman's *hoganda* at Cañon Diablo?"

"Yeah,"—Reeves wiped his slobbering mouth, struggling against Vickers's grip—"yeah, I had to wait till you found out from him where the gal was. I knew he wouldn't tell right out. That ain't an Injun's way. When he said the Snake Dances was being held at Walpi, I knew. Still can't figure how I missed. You must have moved. I placed you dead center before it got too dark. You must have moved."

Vickers shook him again as he started babbling anew. "Who sent you? The Tucson machine?"

"Yeah, yeah." He glanced wild-eyed at the snakes again. "Get me out, Vickers, get me out. The machine. I'll do anything. You promised. The machine. Papago'd worked for us before. We got him to hook the girl so we'd have control over Judge Kern till the elections were over, and we were strong enough to keep the capital at Tucson. Only Papago switched ends on us and brought Sherry here for his own purpose."

"How did you get that handful of fringe from my leggings?"

"Your apprentice printer." Reeves's breathing sounded like a crazed animal's, hoarse, broken. "He cut off a handful when you were sleeping after a bulldog edition. Edgar James had found out about this plot to get Sherry Kern, and had to be eliminated. I guess that's what James meant when he told Sherry your name. You'd been claiming all along the Tucson machine was

49

behind all the trouble in the territory, and James had always laughed at you. It was only then that he knew you were right."

Sherry had turned toward them, a dazed comprehension seeping through the other emotions twisting her face. "You mean Vickers didn't murder Edgar? Why should they try to implicate him at all?"

"I guess you haven't been in the territory long enough to know how Vickers was fighting the Tucson machine," said Reeves. "I guess you don't know how hard they've been trying to get rid of him."

"They've tried it before?" Sherry's voice held doubt.

"I've got a slug in my shoulder for one time," said Vickers in a flat tone. "There's a dead triggerman buried on Caliente Hill for another. I guess they got tired of trying it that way. This was a sort of two-birds-with-one-stone deal, wasn't it?" He jammed Reeves back against the rock wall viciously. "Who was it?"

Reeves's glazed eyes rolled up to him. "When we knew James had to be killed, we paid your apprentice to cut a handful of fringe off your leggings. Everybody knew how you and James hated each other. He made it even better by saying your name at the last . . . ."

"Who was it?"

The utter savagery of Vickers's voice made Reeves recoil. "Papago," he gasped, staring at Vickers. "We'd hired him other times. Papago burned James down." Then he was staring past Vickers. "They're coming. Vickers, you promised. Get me out. Get me out! I can't dance with any snakes. For God's sake!"

Vickers sensed the dancers moving in behind him, and he almost shouted the last, jamming Reeves against the wall. "Who's the top saddle in the machine, Reeves? Who runs the whole thing? You know. Tell me, tell

50

me . . . !"

"No, Vickers, no!" Reeves began fighting with a sudden, bestial fear, screaming and writhing against the rock wall, tearing at Vickers's face, lurching out of his grasp. "Don't let them, Vickers. I ain't going to dance with no snakes. No, Vickers, no . . . !"

Vickers was torn aside from behind, and two Antelope men caught Reeves, pulling him to his feet. Reeves was a big man, his fear giving him a violent strength, and he surged forward with a scream, fighting loose. Another pair of *Moquenos* caught him, and the four dancers shoved the shouting, fighting, man out toward the snakes. When they were near the writhing mass of reptiles, they gave Reeves a last shove. He stumbled forward, unable to catch himself till too late. Already, three of the snakes were coiled. The thump the first one made, striking, carried clearly to Vickers. Reeves's scream was hardly human. Kicking the snakes away, he whirled blindly, but another diamondback whirred and struck. The big man jerked with that hammer blow against his thigh. He tore at the bullet head, whirling and bawling in a frenzy of fear.

"Vickers, get me out! You promised, damn you, promised. Get me out. I ain't going to dance with no snakes. Vickers, Vickers, Vickers!"

The words ended in a crazy scream as another snake hit him. They were all about him now, hissing and rattling and coiling, and he turned this way and that, kicking wildly with his feet, roaring in a terrible fear. Vickers was held spellbound by the ghastly spectacle, filled with a wild impulse to rush in and drag the man out of it, repelled by a growing horror of the snakes. Twice he made a spasmodic move toward Reeves, and the Antelope men caught his arms. Sherry was watching

51

with terrified eyes, bosom rising and falling violently beneath her blouse.

"Vickers, please, Vickers, Vickers." Reeves's shouts became weaker, and he made a last attempt to turn away from the snakes, arms held across his face, and other rattlers struck him, almost knocking him over. He sank to his knees, his cries hoarse, pitiful, shaking and blubbering. He tried to crawl out on his hands and knees. Another snake coiled before him, hissing, rattling. Reeves let out a last, hoarse scream, rising almost to his feet. Turning wildly away, he shuddered at its blow, falling down again.

He sank onto his belly, his soft blubbering becoming incoherent, finally stopping, to lie there, a great hulk of a man in his Levi's and red flannels, utterly silent.

Two Antelope men walked out to get him. A rattler struck at one of them, and he kicked the snake away casually, stooping to lift Reeves. They carried him back past Vickers into the room from which they had come.

Vickers caught himself abruptly, moving over till Sherry was against his side, catching her cold hand. "You've got to trust Fallon. It's our only chance, Sherry. It was the panic that got Reeves. Not the snakes. A man doesn't die that fast from their bite. Maybe fear makes the venom work faster. I don't know. All I know is you can't let it affect you like that. Fallon said he'd get us out. Do you hear me, Sherry?"

"I hear you, Vickers." Her voice was small, shaky. She was trembling against him, and her fingers dug into his palm till the nails brought blood. Then a *tombe* began to beat from the nearby rooftop.

In front of the *kee-si* was a pit dug in the ground, supposed to represent *Shi-pa-pu*, the Black Lake of Tears, and the twenty men of the Antelope Society

52

began circling this, shaking their *guajes*. Then a huge *tombe* on the rooftop nearby began to beat, and the men of the Snake Society emerged from the sacred *estufa* at the north end of the court. The captain of the Snake Society, upon reaching the first snake, tickled it with a feather as it started to coil, making it stretch out, then snatched it behind the head and put it between his teeth. A man of the Antelope Society placed his arm around the snake-man's shoulders, and together they started in the peculiar hippety-hop toward the sacred rock at the south end of the court. Each snake-man in turn took his snake, and was joined by his Antelope partner. As the third pair left the *kee-si* together, an Antelope man emerged from the booth behind them, so close that Vickers was sure he alone saw it, the Indians on the rooftops probably not even aware the man had not been there all the time, the dancers too busy with their rituals to notice where he came from. There were seventeen of the Snake Society, and twenty of the Antelope, and when they had all paired off, it left three Antelope Men to gather up the snakes as each pair of dancers rounded the sacred dancing rock and came back, each snake-man dropping his reptile with a twist of his head. The snakes were writhing furiously in the *Moquenos'* mouths now, trying desperately to strike the Indians, all their leverage for striking dissipated by the position in which they hung. The captain of the Snake Society had already rid himself of his first snake, and standing by the *kee-si* with his partner, rattled his ceremonial *guaje* at the whites, calling something.

"What did he say?" Sherry's voice was hoarse.

"He's ordering us to pick up a snake and dance with it in our mouth," said Vickers.

Suddenly the girl's body was shuddering violently.

53

Her teeth showed white against her red lower lip, drawing blood, and her voice shook with the terrible effort she was making to control herself.

"I can't do this," she said. "I can't. I can't!"

"You've got to," said Vickers tensely. The Antelope man who had come from the booth was separating a big diamondback from three other reptiles on the courtyard floor. He reached in with both hands to grab the snake behind its head before it could coil. Vickers saw a smaller one coil and strike, and saw the man flinch and grit his teeth.

Fallon. Dressed in the bizarre costume, he moved toward them, holding the leaping diamondback, two red dots on his right hand. Sweat was streaking the black paint on his face.

"Take it," he told Sherry under his breath. "It's the one I fixed. Take it."

Sherry stumbled backward, her hands out in front of her, face pale. Vickers clamped his teeth shut and grabbed the snake behind the head, just beneath Fallon's grip, tearing it from him. He caught Sherry by the arm, pulling her violently to him, then caught her abundance of black hair and held her head rigid, her body against him, and jammed the seven feet of writhing serpent against her face. She screamed, and for that moment her face was twisted in utter horror. Then he felt her stiffen against him, and her eyes were staring wide and suddenly free from fear into his, and it was as if she took the strength from him.

Her mouth opened, and he forced the snake between her teeth, and she bit into the smooth, diamond-marked hide so hard the tail and head leaped into the air, the circle of paint Fallon had daubed on its body near the rattles gleaming wetly. An Antelope man put his arm

54

around Sherry and guided her toward the dancing rock in that strange hippety-hop.

Fallon had already chosen another marked snake for Vickers. Vickers felt a moment of sick revulsion and closed his eyes as he took the snake from Fallon's hand, jamming it into his mouth. It tasted wet and acrid and sandy all at once, and he almost gagged on it. The fetid arm of a sweating Antelope man was thrown around his shoulder, and they hopped toward the dancing rock. The snake beat against him, sending waves of nausea through his whole body, and he knew an insupportable desire to vomit.

But as he turned the dancing rock with the stinking partner, he saw the real danger was ahead of them. The snakes which the other pairs had dropped were slithering across the courtyard between the rock and the *kee-si*, and, although the three Antelope men relegated to that job kept picking them up and putting them into the cottonwood booth, there were always some snakes left on the ground.

Sherry and the Antelope man who was dancing with her were almost to the *kee-si* when she dropped the snake from her mouth. It slithered away, and she tried to disengage herself from the Antelope man. Vickers could see it now, and almost upset the man hopping with him as he tried to reach Sherry. One of the diamondbacks had freed itself from the writhing mass on the floor within the circle of dancers, slithering directly toward Sherry and her partner, and it had no paint daubed on its tail.

Vickers dropped his own snake, fighting free of his partner, leaping toward her, as the diamondback reared up, and coiled. Sherry screamed, scratching the face of her partner, but he caught her hand, ignoring the coiling

55

snake to pull her toward the *kee-si* to get another serpent. A sob escaped Vickers as he saw that he would be too late. The diamondback's head disappeared in a blur of movement. Vickers shouted in a hoarse, cracked way, still running forward. Then he saw what had happened. Somehow, another Antelope man had gotten in between Sherry and the snake in that last instant, and the serpent fell back from striking the man's leg.

"Fallon," gasped Vickers between his teeth, and suddenly understood what the man had meant back in the *kiva*. *I'll see that they don't bite you.*

Again the *Moquenos* made them take snakes in their mouths, and again it was Fallon who managed to be the one handing them each a snake, picking out the ones marked with paint. This time Sherry took it herself. She was sobbing and her hands were shaking, but she took the ugly reptile, making a choked sound as she forced it into her mouth, and started dancing toward the rock again. Fallon caught a snake for Vickers, staggering toward him. The man's face was turned muddy by the sweat mixing with the black paint, and he fell against Vickers, gasping.

"We're doing it, we're doing it. If only she can hang on one more time. Three times around, see . . . ."

After the third time to the rock and back again, after casting aside the writhing snake, Vickers asked him: "Why, Fallon?"

"My job, isn't it?" panted Fallon, shoving him. "I'm all right. Got hold of some of that tea they call *mah-que-he*. Antelope men drink it to give them immunity. Kern sent me out to get her, didn't he?"

"This isn't your job," said Vickers, fighting with the writhing snake in his grasp. "A man wouldn't do this just for a job. You knew what it meant. You knew that

56

*mah-que-he* wouldn't give you immunity. These snake-men train all their lives. They've been drinking that tea eight days now. You knew what it meant. Why, Fallon?"

Fallon whirled to face him fully, those wide eyes meeting his, a little crazy now. "You know why! You came for the same reason. Even when I met you there in the Tortillas, it had already happened to you. Just hearing about her. I knew her, see. You just heard about her, and it happened to you. I knew her. That's why!"

The *tombe* stopped. A hush fell over the throng on the walls, and the sweating dancers halted, drawing together in front of the *kee-si*. The captain of the Snake Society held up his *guaje*, turning toward the four quarters, then bowing to Vickers.

"Abeïto spoke the truth. No *pahanas* has ever passed the ordeal before you. The Trues have sent you."

Vickers had a chance to speak with Fallon, grabbing his arm when they passed him going out. "You're coming with us. If you can't get away now, we'll wait for you below."

"Don't be a fool," said Fallon. "I can't leave till the dance is over. They'd suspect something."

"Fallon . . . ."

"No!" The man jerked away, his face twisted. "This tea's about through working in me anyway. You know that. What's the use of risking your life for a dead man? I did this for her. You get her back. Promise me that!"

Vickers drew a heavy breath. "I promise you that."

"Now, get the hell out of here!"

They gave Vickers his Henry back, and the roan Fallon had taken at Cañon Diablo, and another horse for Sherry. The *Moquenos* watched them pass down the street, sullen and silent, and Vickers could see how

57

many of them were still drunk on Reeves's whiskey. He was practically holding Sherry up, and, as they neared the start of the trail down, leading their horses, he felt her grow taut against him, and he saw it, too.

They were strung out across the trail, a dozen or more, with their narrow, drunken faces and glittering eyes and .50 Sharps, and Papago stood out in front of them. "You aren't taking the girl, Vickers. Hand her over, and you can go."

"I'm taking her, Papago. You heard the decision of the *principales*. You'll be bucking more than me, if you try to stop us."

"The *Moquenos* won't interfere," said Papago. "You see how drunk they are. They'd just as soon see you dead as not, after the way you messed up their Snake Dance. Now, hand her over."

"It won't stop with me," said Vickers. "There's still the Tucson machine. Do you think Reeves will be the last man they send up here?"

"As a matter of fact," said Papago, "I do."

"You're dreaming," said Vickers.

"No," said Papago, "you wanted to know who sat the top saddle in the Tucson machine? A strong man, Vickers. The kind of man who could get out and do something himself when his men failed."

The implication of that shocked Vickers enough to take him off guard, and his incredulity was in his voice. "Are you trying to say that Reeves . . . ?"

" . . . was the head of the Tucson machine! He'd sent half a dozen of his men out to find the girl before he finally got impatient and came himself. He was that kind, Vickers. Almost as dangerous as you. And now that he's gone, Kern won't have much trouble shifting the capital back to Prescott and smashing the machine

58

for good." Papago shifted impatiently. "I'm through talking. Come on alone, and we'll let you do it standing up."

"You're bluffing, Papago," said Vickers. "You don't dare defy the edict of the *principales*, if you want them to help you against the troops. We're coming through."

He put one hand behind Sherry's back, guided her forward, but with his first move Papago went for his gun. "This is how we're bluffing, Vickers."

Vickers had not really believed they would try it here. He could have brought his own Henry up and cocked it about the same time Papago got the Remington out, but that would have left Sherry in the line of fire. With a grunt, he threw himself against the girl, not even trying for his own gun, and the two of them went down, rolling into the dark doorway of the adobe house on this side, the roar of gunfire echoing down the street as Papago and the Apaches opened up.

The wall cut him off from most of the Apaches, but he could still see two of them out there. He snapped the lever of his Henry, and it bucked in his hand, and one Apache yelled and doubled over, dropping his Sharps. A new volley of gunfire rocked the narrow way, and bullets made their deadly thud into the mud walls all about Vickers. But there were only one or two Apaches beside Papago with six-shooters, and the others had those old, single-shot Sharps rifles. The sudden cessation of gun-sound told him they had emptied their rifles and had to take that moment for reloading, and he knew it would be his only chance.

"There's only one way to finish this," he muttered.

"Papago?" said Sherry.

He turned to see her face, pale and drawn in the dim light, staring up at him. "Indians are like that, Sherry.

59

Get their leader and all the sand will go out of them."

"Vickers, you can't go out there . . . ."

"I can," said Vickers. "While they're busy with me, you get out of here and back down the street to the *principales*. They'll keep their word about letting you go."

"Vickers . . . ."

But he was already throwing himself out the door with his Henry held across his belly, an adamantine cast to his lean, burned face, his mouth twisting as he saw the first Apache skulking down the wall across the street, and fired. The man jerked against the wall, still trying to jam a fresh load down his Sharps, then fell forward onto his face. A figure loomed on the roof of the first level across the street, and Vickers realized they had been trying to come up on him inside the house that way. The man had a six-gun and began firing wildly, with both hands, and only then did Vickers recognize him. The Henry made its single hollow boom.

"I told you, Combabi, I told you," shouted Vickers, still going forward down the street, as Combabi pitched head foremost off the roof, and then Vickers's eyes swung to the man farther down in the middle of the street. He had been trying to work down next to the wall while Vickers was inside, but, as soon as Vickers showed, he had moved into the center. It was some distance, and Papago did not fire as most Indians would have. He moved toward Vickers, increasing his speed, bent forward a little. Vickers was still turning from firing at Combabi, and he snapped the lever home hard, and the gun bucked hot against his belly. Papago did not jerk, and Vickers knew he had missed. Then Papago's Remington spoke.

Vickers had been shot before, and the hammer blow

60

against his leg was no new sensation. The street seemed to drop from beneath him, and he found himself on his belly with the Henry pinned beneath him. A terrible, swimming pain robbed him of all volition. Through a haze he saw Papago still coming forward, lining up the gun for another shot. Then it was Sherry's voice.

"Vickers!"

Something inside him grew taut and hard and clear. He pulled the gun upward till the barrel lay beneath his chin, snapping the cylinder out sideways beneath him. Papago saw it and tried to stop him, firing sooner than he had intended. The hard earth kicked up in a puff of acrid, blinding dust before Vickers's eyes. He squeezed the trigger that way.

When the dust fell and the stunning force of the bullet striking earth so near to Vickers left him, he could see Papago, lying on his belly down the street. The Apaches were already beginning to gather about their leader, forgetting Vickers. One of them had a surprised look on his face. Then it was Sherry's hands on Vickers, soft, cool, somehow, lifting him up. The pain in his leg made him dizzy.

"Help me on the roan," he said between gritted teeth. "We've got to get out. It's all over now."

She helped him up against the horse, her arms about his body. "In a way it's over, Vickers, but in another way, it's just begun," she said "I told you I didn't think you were crazy, back in that room. You were right. It can happen that way . . . to a man"—and her eyes were soft and smoky, meeting his—"or a woman."

61

# THE LASH OF
# *SEÑORITA* SCORPION

*This short novel continues the adventures of Elgera Douglas, better known as Señorita Scorpion. The first three short novels about this character are collected in chronological order in **The Legend of Señorita Scorpion** (Circle Ⓥ Westerns, 1996) and a fourth short novel about her, "The Curse of Montezuma," is to be found in **The Return of Señorita Scorpion** (Circle Ⓥ Westerns, 1997). In the earlier stories, although both Chisos Owens and Johnny Hagar are in love with Elgera, those romances are never consummated. Savage's original title for this short novel was "The Return of Señorita Scorpion," and it was accepted by Fiction House in early March, 1947, and on March 11th the author was paid $500.00 for it, approximately 2½¢ a word. The story was titled for publication "Lash of the Six-Gun Queen," and it was supposed to appear in the Fall, 1947 issue of **Action Stories**. In fact, the oil painting to be used on the cover for that issue had already been ordered from the graphic illustrator, Allen Anderson, and this painting did appear on the cover of the Fall, 1947 issue. What didn't appear in that issue was the new Señorita Scorpion novel. It was published, instead, in the Winter, 1947 issue. In this continuation of the saga Les Savage, Jr., added a new character in the form of the first-person narrator, U. S. Marshal Powder Welles. At the time, Savage had begun experimenting with first-person narration in his Western stories, very much under the sway of Raymond*

62

*Chandler's detective stories then in vogue, written in a style noted for its flamboyant and vivid similes and metaphors, enriching the imagery with the patois of highly-stylized American slang and supposedly underworld parlance. While there was a certain novelty to these attempts by Savage, the author later abandoned this approach, and Welles never returns in later stories in the saga. Also by the time Savage came to write this short novel, he was making ample use of Ramon F. Adams's seminal **Western Words: A Dictionary of the Range, Cow Camp, and Trail**, first published in book form by the University of Oklahoma Press in 1944. These expressions, unfamiliar perhaps to some modern readers, are coin of the realm in that reference book. For its advent in book form here the text of this short novel has been restored, according to the author's original typescript.*

# I

BUTCHERKNIFE HILL WAS ABOUT THIRTY MILES NORTH of the Mexican border, and they had told me in Alpine I would find him there. The first thing I thought, upon seeing him, was bull. That's exactly the way it bulged into my mind. Bull. And you don't know what that means really, unless you've seen a real, old-time mossyhorn sulking. Pure destruction with its tail switching. Shoulders so big and flanks so small he looks out of shape, almost awkward, till he moves. Cats don't have more grace. But he doesn't have to move. Just look in those little red eyes, and you've got it.

"Chisos Owens?" I said.

His eyes weren't red, though. They were the color of gunsmoke. He sat a big dun with an arched mane, and

63

his Porter rig was double-girted the way all Texas men like them. His Levi's and old cotton shirt were so faded and soiled I couldn't tell the original color.

"Marshal Powder Welles?" he said. He had thin lips for such a heavy-boned face, and they barely moved over the words.

"News travels fast in the Big Bend," I said.

"We have a grapevine of sorts," he told me. "I heard you were in Alpine, inquiring after me. I don't know where the Scorpion is, Marshal, and, if I did, I wouldn't tell you."

My own Porter rig creaked as I leaned toward him. "That was a United States senator the Scorpion murdered in Alpine, Owens. I work for the same government. Do I have to tell you the trouble you are going to get in for not helping me, or are we going somewhere and talk?"

The back of his hand was covered with pale blond hair, except where an old rope burn cut across it. He put his fingers around the saddle horn. There was a faint, distinct popping sound. It must have come from the cords on his wrist, standing out as big as dally ropes in that moment with the force of his grip. Then he lifted his shoulders in a shrug and led the way up to a line shack on the ridge. There was a cottonwood corral out back, and we turned our animals in there. A plank table and a pair of pegged-pine benches made up the furniture inside, with wall bunks at the rear and an old wood stove in one corner. He threw some chunks of mesquite on and filled the coffee pot from the water butt inside the door. I sat down at the table and took off my John B. to scratch my head.

"It's funny how the Mexicans tack on names like that," I said. "*Señorita* Scorpion. I understand it fits

64

Elgera Douglas."

"It fits," he said.

"I understand you were in love with her."

He was turned away from me, when I said it, and bent over the stove. But his whole great frame seemed to lift a little with the breath he took. Finally he turned around and lowered himself to the bench opposite me. He put those rope-burned hands on the table in front of him and took one fist in the other hand and cracked the knuckles, staring at them.

"What do you want to know?" he asked.

"Where *Señorita* Scorpion is," I told him.

"I'll show that card just once more," he said. "I don't know where she is."

"I guess you know why Senator Bailes was down this way," I told him.

"I'm out of touch, down here," he answered.

"It looks like this war with Spain is the real thing," I explained. "Teddy Roosevelt's Rough Riders are going to need a lot of horses. Government's commissioned horse runners all over the country to gather in the wildest horses for the cavalry. Some enterprising young mustanger has been going below the border for his animals, and he hasn't been too particular whether they're mustangs or broke horses he brings back. Activity seems to center around the Big Bend, and it seems like none of the state officers has been very effective in checking it. The Mexican government told Washington, if they didn't send someone responsible down, it was going to raise a helluva ruckus. Even mention of war.

"So Senator Warren Bailes came down to see what was up with the local authorities and try to get some action out of them. He must have dug up something

65

good. Washington had got word they'd see the end of it in a few days. The morning after he sent the wire, Bailes stepped out onto the corner of First and Main in your fair county seat, and in bulges this Scorpion on her buttermilk hoss and empties every blue whistler in her dewey right through Senator Warren Bailes."

His eyes had taken on a smoky color, and he was staring past me, almost talking to himself. "The worst part of it is, Elgera is so capable of it. I wouldn't believe it. I still don't want to. But she is so capable of it. Get her mad and she. . . ."

He lifted his head with a jerk, as if realizing the release. His eyes moved to me, and they looked even more like a sulking bull's now. He cracked his knuckles again. That irritated me somehow.

"I don't know how out of touch you are," I said. "You seem to have a pretty busy line between here and Alpine. Where's Johnny Hagar?"

I've questioned enough men to know the value of snubbing them up like that. The unexpectedness of it lifted his head again that way. The Arbuckle's started boiling over, and he got up and moved the pot off the open blaze. They'd said he was hard to rile, but there was a stiff line to his shoulders, and I wondered how much farther along the fence I could push him.

"The Douglas faction, they call it," I said. "More machine, from what I hear, with Johnny Hagar county sheriff and you town marshal in Alpine, and Elgera Douglas sitting on the county board. Striker's bunch didn't have much chance in those days, did they? What is it, Owens? What did Senator Bailes find that threatened the set-up you and the Scorpion have? How is she tied into this mustang business?"

There was a tinny clatter. I didn't see it for a moment.

66

Then he backed away to reveal the coffee pot overturned on the stove and all that good Arbuckle's spreading out like ink on the floor.

"Tetchy, aren't you, for a man that doesn't know anything?" I said.

"Listen." He turned to me, and he held his knuckles again. I kept waiting for them to pop. Crazy how something like that can get on your nerves. "Listen, Welles, marshal or not, you'd better go now. I don't know where Elgera Douglas is. I don't know where Johnny Hagar is. I don't know anything. You'd better go."

I scratched my head again. "Texas Stock Association. Is that the T.S.A. brand on those cattle you're herding?"

I didn't think he would answer for a minute. "Used to be the Scorpion's beef," he said finally, wheezing a little like a man with a bullet wound. "The courts are holding her estate till this thing is cleared up. T.S.A. is handling the beef for the courts."

"You've got a rep as a lone wolf," I said. "Like to rod your own cut. Never favored the big combines. You don't look right in this chorus, somehow. Why did you sign on with T.S.A.?"

He was getting more and more like a bull. It came out of him with a sort of groaning sound. "Welles. . . ."

"Maybe you don't know Kelley Striker is the president of T.S.A.'s board of directors," I told him. "I can't figure a man like you signing onto an outfit rodded by the same *hombre* who kicked you and Hagar out of the wagon the minute Elgera Douglas's support was gone. Is there something under the soogan here, Owens, or did your guts leak out when the Scorpion bought a trunk?"

"Damn you!" he yelled, and through the yell I could

67

hear his knuckles crack again, and that was the tip-off.

He came right across the table at me. If I hadn't already started to jump up and kick the bench back away from beneath my feet, I would have been pinned beneath the table and Owens, because his lunge had tipped it over. He and the furniture crashed over onto the floor. One of his hands struck my side beneath my ribs. For just an instant I felt the awesome strength of him. I couldn't help yelling with the pain of those pinching fingers. Then I had torn loose, going on back, and he had tumbled to the floor.

He got up with blinding speed for such a hulk, and his legs were bent to jump me where I stood against the wall. Then he stopped, with all his weight thrown forward on his toes, hands outstretched, staring at the old Cloverleaf house gun in my hand.

"Really hell with the hide off, aren't you?" I said. "I guess I'd better tell you why I really came. Spanish Jack was going to send one of his own deputies, but I wanted a talk with you anyway, so he let me serve this subpoena on you. It's for your appearance at another inquest they're holding on Senator Bailes's death next Monday. Now, shall we go for our hay-burners, or do you want to dig up a tomahawk?"

## II

IT WAS ABOUT SIXTY MILES FROM THE BORDER TO Alpine, and Butcherknife Hill lay just about halfway between. It was hotter than the hinges of hell through those thirty miles between Butcherknife and the county seat, and my pied mare was played clear out by the time we rode in past the Southern Pacific's brick dépôt and cattle chutes at the end of Main. Si Samson's Livery, it

68

said on the peeling sign above the big double doors of a barn on the corner of Second and Main. Si looked like a bronco-slashed hand. He was all bent over and had a painful limp, and his hair was hogged as short and stiff as the mane on Owens's dun. He stopped when he saw us, staring at Chisos Owens.

"Judas," he said.

"What do you mean?" I asked him.

"Nothing," said Si, looking down at the ground. "Nothing. You gentlemen want to stall your animals here? Looks like they need a good rubdown. Have my boy do it for fifty cents extra."

I stepped off Pie and unlashed my saddle roll from behind the cantle. Summer dust was the color of a dirty dun horse in the street, and I had the feeling that the old man was standing in the doorway of his barn and watching us till we reached the opposite side. The Alpine Lodge was a big frame building on this corner with a wooden overhang shading the sidewalk. There was the usual line of idlers. The idleness dropped off them like a kak with the cinch cut, when we passed across the porch. I was in the lobby before I heard one of the chairs scrape. The plank walk made a hollow, wooden plump that receded southward.

Owens and I cleaned up, then went downstairs to the grub house next door. Cecile's Café, it said, and had as strong a smell inside as most of those greasy-sack outfits you find in a border town. I forgot the smell when Cecile came out of the kitchen.

Have you ever seen nopal after a spring rain? That's how red Cecile's lips were. Eyes that gave you the same feeling as when you look into a deep pool of cool water on a blistering day. The gingham dress was stamped with blue flowers and had built-in curves. She didn't do

69

anything as obvious as Si Samson. But I caught the momentary hesitation, about halfway down the counter toward us, as she recognized him. Then she came on.

"Chisos," she said, a little breathlessly. "Haven't seen you for ages."

"Cecile?" I asked.

"Cecile Peters," Owens said. "Marshal Welles."

"How long have you known Chisos?" I asked her.

"Long time, Marshal," she told me. "Menu?"

"That's funny," I said. "When you first came in, you looked like you'd never seen anything quite like him before."

She made a little pout with her mouth, handing Owens a menu, too, but I wouldn't let it go. I put my elbows down and leaned forward, pinning my eyes on her.

"Si Samson had the same look. So did the clerk in the Alpine Lodge. What is it, Cecile? Didn't they expect Chisos was coming back with me?"

Her smiled began at one corner of her lips, not all humor, something almost wistful, and built slow, and her eyes slid around to Owens. "Maybe that's it, Marshal," she said softly.

"Bryce Wylie was the deputy Spanish Jack told me he meant to send with that subpoena," I said.

Auburn lights rippled through her hair with the negative shake of her head, and her eyes were still on Owens.

"Spanish Jack?" I asked her.

"I don't think even he could have done it," she said. "As a matter of fact, I don't think there is any man in Alpine who would have wanted to try and bring Chisos Owens in, except maybe Johnny Hagar, and he's not here any more."

70

"What were the odds on the opera seat?" I asked.

She looked at me, and the smile was full now. "As a matter of fact, they *were* making bets. The boys in front of the Alpine Lodge were offering odds five to one against your bringing Chisos back."

It made me mad at first, to realize how I'd been used by Spanish Jack, and then, somehow, I had to laugh. I heard the cracking sound beside me. It was Owens, with his knuckles.

"All right," he growled. "How about eating?"

"I'm right sorry, Chisos. I didn't know. I wouldn't have showed you up in front of your girl this way for the world."

"I'm not his girl," said Cecile.

I glanced up suddenly at her eyes, because she and Owens were looking at each other again, and that thing was between them. I was close enough to see the color, now. Blue. A deep, dark blue. Then the roots of her hair. She sensed it and turned toward me.

"What would you suggest?" I asked, tapping the menu.

"The beef stew is particularly flavorable, Marshal." It seemed deep for her voice. Then I saw her mouth was closed, and where she was looking. Tension stiffened the deep planes of muscle across Owens's back, lifting his shoulders up till he looked like he was bent over. I turned on the stool. It was Spanish Jack, standing behind us.

He was almost too handsome. He had a head of hair so black it looked blue, thick and curly as mesquite grass. Even the burnsides were curly. His skin was swarthy but so clear and fine his cheekbones under the light gleamed through it like an Indian's, and his teeth were as white as the polished bone handle on my house

71

gun.

I jerked my thumb at Owens. "Here's your chestnut."

Jack made a little motion with one womanish hand. It gave me the sense of leaves fluttering. "Chestnut?" he said, frowning.

I looked at one of my own hands. "My fingers aren't burned, either. Did you lose any money, Sheriff?"

Jack turned to look at Bryce Wylie who had entered behind him. The deputy was a big, kettle-bellied man in the sloppy serge vest and pants of what must have once been a pretty good suit. He packed a *buscadero* gun belt, and it creaked a little as he hooked his thumbs on it and pressed down heavily, shrugging at Jack. The lawman turned back, trying to make his smile at Cecile easy.

"I told you he was a salty character," he said.

"Yeah," I said, "so full of alkali my uppers are rusty. This another one of your boys?"

The smile faded as he glanced to the other side where a third man now stood. "Yes, Marshal, Jerry Hammer. A good boy. Meet Marshal Welles, Jerry."

"Gladtameetcha, Marshal," he said.

It was interesting to see how much humor he could keep out of his empty little eyes with such a big smile on his mouth. He had that rolling bulge to his heavy thighs you get in a short man sometimes, and it had split the seams out on his buckskin *chivarras*. His upper body was the same way, looking like they'd piled on the muscles till they couldn't any more, and his white cotton shirt had trouble containing him. His nose had been broken badly, and there was a deep scar the color of raw liver cutting through the greasy blue stubble of one cheek.

"You look like you've had a hard life, Hammer," I

72

said. I might as well have reached out and wiped that smile from his lips with my hand, the way it disappeared.

Spanish Jack formed a laugh. "We'll take Owens off your hands now, Welles. Did he cause you any bother?"

"If I had a bet on it, I would've worried about it more," I said. "What do you mean . . . take him off my hands?"

I saw Cecile stiffen a little behind the counter.

"Till the inquest, of course," said Jack.

"He was never on my hands," I said. "That was a subpoena I served on him, not a warrant."

"Yes, of course, of course," said Jack.

Owens had not turned around yet. His shoulders were still hunched forward that way.

Jack looked at him. "Coming, Chisos?"

"Wait a minute, Jack," I said. "Where are you taking him?"

"To the jail," said the sheriff. "We'll hold him in custody till the inquest."

"You said Judge Kerreway is holding the inquest," I reminded him. "He's coming all the way from Marathon to do it. Is he staying with friends?"

Spanish Jack didn't want to get his feet in these oxbows, and it began to prey on him. "What are you getting at, Marshal?" he asked, a little furrow appearing between his pretty brows.

"The judge isn't registered at the Alpine Lodge," I told him. "You couldn't hold the inquest without him, could you?"

"Not exactly. Perhaps he was held up."

"I paid an extra dollar for a double at the Lodge, and I'm not going to throw that away for nothing. I think you better let Chisos Owens sleep there tonight. If

73

there's an inquest, he'll be at it."

"I want to make sure he'll be at it," said Jack. "Come on, Chisos."

"Don't try to put this bronco in the chute, Jack," I told him. "It's too narrow."

"I'm taking him," he said.

"Have you got a warrant, Sheriff?"

"I don't need one."

"Then you're not taking him officially?"

"I'm taking him. Come on, Chisos."

"Marshal . . . !" This last was as shrill as a maverick calf bawling for milk, coming from Cecile, and she never finished it, because Jack had stepped forward to grab Owens's shoulder and try and pull him around. Owens came around all right, more of his own volition than Jack's. After that it all went so fast I didn't rightly take everything in.

Owens's spinning motion whirled him off the stool into Spanish Jack with his head down and those bull shoulders in Jack's middle. It carried Jack backward. Jerry Hammer pulled a gun and lunged forward to whip Owens across the back of the neck while he was still bent forward.

"Well, hell . . . ," I told them and went in on it, dragging at my own dewey. But there was Wylie. I was suddenly blocked off by his body. He got one hand around my right wrist before I had my Cloverleaf pulled free. The palm felt like sandpaper, and I thought my bones would crumble in the grip. His body carried me right back to where I'd come from. I knocked aside the stool I'd jumped off of and crashed into the counter so hard it knocked a dirty plate off farther down.

Suddenly the whole Big Dipper was inside my head, each star flashing on and off separately. I found myself

74

sitting on the floor with my back against the counter and those sloppy serge pants in front of me and realized dimly he must have smashed me full in the face.

He lifted a foot to kick me. I caught it in both hands and rolled to one side. The jerk took him off balance. Before he hit the floor, I was on my feet, pawing for a stool. I couldn't see very well yet. Things were still spinning, and something thick and wet kept getting in my eyes. But I caught his movement to rise. I took the stool by its seat and jammed the legs at Wylie. He howled and tried to get away. I jumped after his rolling body, jamming the legs in when his face came around again. His screams sounded like a loco horse, and I figured I'd gotten his eyes.

"Marshal . . . Marshal . . . !"

With Cecile crying like that from somewhere, I dropped the stool and spun toward the others. Jerry Hammer was probably the only man in the room who could have closed with Chisos Owens and kept up his own end. The two of them were in the middle of the room, slugging it out. Beyond them, where Owens's first lunge must have knocked him, was Spanish Jack, just getting to his hands and knees in a corner. I figured what was in his mind and was already jumping past Owens and Hammer when Jack's fingers made that fluttering motion.

He was still on his knees as I reached him. I kicked the Colt from his hand just as it cleared leather. It skidded across the floor. He dove past me, after the gun, with a hoarse shout. I had to spin around to catch him. He had his hand on the Colt again. I don't do more walking than I can help, and my heels were still pretty well spiked. Wylie's screams became puny compared to Spanish Jack's when I stamped down.

75

There was a crash from behind me like a bunch of freight cars, coming to a quick stop. Jack was through for the moment, and I turned to see. Owens had knocked Jerry Hammer across the counter, and a whole shelf full of dishes had fallen down on him. Hammer didn't get out from under the wreckage.

Owens started rubbing the back of his neck, looking at Spanish Jack where he lay huddled on the floor, holding that mangled hand and groaning, and then at Bryce Wylie, sitting against the counter farther down with his hands over his face. Finally Chisos Owens looked at me, and stopped rubbing his neck.

"Snuffy little bronco, ain't you?" he said mildly.

### III

SOME OPERA-SEAT ARGUFIER SAID THERE WERE ONLY two things the old-time cowhand really feared—being set afoot and a decent woman—and that he'd do anything to keep from calling a spade a spade in front of the latter. That's how a bull came to be called a duke. And here was the duke again, filling the room with that switching, pawing, snorting destruction, pacing from one wall to the other, his shoulders so big and his hips so small that his hips acted as a swivel to swing his upper body from side to side every time he took a step.

"Why should Jack want to get hold of you so bad?" I asked.

Owens stopped pacing at our hotel window that overlooked Main. "I don't know."

We had left Spanish Jack and his deputies to do their own cleaning up down at Cecile's. I had some cleaning up of my own to do. My face felt like a bronco had stamped it, and it looked that way in the cracked mirror.

76

I poured some water from the cracked china pitcher into the cracked washbowl.

"I really didn't think Spanish Jack would buck a government man that way," I told Owens. "He must really think he's in a fancy kak, pulling a high-heel time like that."

"Jack is Striker's man," said Owens, "and Striker practically owns the Big Bend."

"They aren't bigger than the U. S. government," I said. "I suppose I could swear out a formal complaint, or call in the military, but that would snub things up too tight. I'd like to give them a little more rope. I've sent a wire to Judge Kerreway in Marathon, and, if he really hasn't been called in to sit on a second inquest, that will put a new rigging on this horse. What you got, Chisos, that they want so bad?"

"Nothing," he said. "I don't know."

"What did you think you'd find out, signing up with T.S.A.?"

He turned to look at me. His eyes met mine in the glass. For a minute that sullen, powdery color filled them. Then I saw the pattern of crow's feet around the edges. It might have all been from weathering, or he might have been studying something. He moved over toward me, still watching my face in the glass.

"What do you mean to do . . . when you find the Scorpion?" he asked.

"My duty would be to bring her in and turn her over to the proper authorities," I said. "How much of a chance do you want me to give her?"

He took an impatient breath, turning back. "I'm mixed up, Marshal. For the first time in my life, I'm mixed up. I've always been able to ride straight down the trail before. When things got in my way, I got them

77

out of it in one manner or another. But I'm up against a fence here, and it's hog-tight and horse-high and bull-strong, and I can't get through. I saw her do it. I was standing right down there on the corner of Second and Main when Senator Bailes came out of the Alpine, and I saw her ride up on that palomino and empty her gun into him, and ride away."

"And you can't quite believe it."

He shook his head. "I'll believe she shot him. I know Elgera. But there's something wrong."

"Wasn't Kelly Striker the campaign manager for Bailes when he was running for the Senate?" I asked.

I saw him nod in the mirror.

I wiped my hands on the bloody towel. "I'll give the woman the same chance I gave you, Chisos," I said.

He turned again, and there were those crow's feet. "Just why did you jump in down there? You put your foot in a deeper bog than you realize. Spanish Jack won't forget it, and Striker's a big man. He might even have the power to touch you."

"I didn't like the length of Jack's burnsides," I said.

Owens laughed suddenly. It was the first time I'd heard him do it. "All right, Marshal," he said. "When I told you I didn't know where Elgera is, I meant it. But there are a few leads. That palomino of hers, La Rubia she calls it, The Blonde. Nobody else could ride it. A Mexican friend of mine claims he saw it without a rider down by the Dead Horse Mountains. That's near the Lost Santiago Valley. Not many people could find her, if she was hiding out in her old home. I've been to the valley myself a couple of times lately and didn't come across any sign that she was there. But if you want to have a look-see, I'll take you."

"That would make me as happy as a red bangtail in a

78

Porter kak."

Ⓥ Ⓥ Ⓥ Ⓥ Ⓥ

Sierra del Caballo Muerto, they called them, the Mountains of the Dead Horse, because some Spaniards had got lost there in the old days, and they and their horses had all died through lack of water. I thought I'd seen some badlands in my time, but they were the Promised Land compared to this. There were trees, sometimes, but they didn't pack any more spinach than you could grow on a slick horn. There were riverbeds, but they hadn't been wet since a hundred years before the first Comanche burnt *sotol* stalks in rimrock. There was *toboso* grass, but it was so tough even the buffaloes had let it alone.

Buzzards floated on air so still that it hurt my ears, and they must have been waiting up there a long time for us, because I couldn't see anything else alive enough to die. My pied horse was ganted up like a heifer with the Spanish fever, and I had to get off every half hour or so and wipe the alkali out of his nose so he wouldn't choke to death.

There ain't no hoss that cain't be rode.
There ain't no man that cain't be throwed.

"Will you shut up?" Chisos Owens said. "There ain't no cause to sing. We're just about at the entrance to Crimson Cañon. It leads into the Lost Santiago Mine. The mine goes clean through this hogback of the Dead Horses into Santiago Valley. If you want to turn back, now's your chance. From here on it's touch and go."

"Let's go, then," I told him.

79

He stepped off his dun and unslung a pair of old *armitas* he had hitched to his saddle horn. He buckled these hide aprons on and got a pair of gloves from his saddle roll. I saw why in a few minutes. The cañon walls were as red as rot-gut bourbon, and so narrow we were riding in shadow dark as night at two in the afternoon.

Soon the way became so choked with prickly pear and horse-maiming cactus and mesquite we could hardly force our way through. Coming from the north, I wasn't even prepared by as much as having *tapaderos* on my stirrups. The thorny brush kept tearing my boots out of the oxbows and ripping holes in my Levi's and gouging my hands till I was ornery enough to eat horseshoes. Owens didn't pay any attention, and finally we reached the end and, sure enough, pushing our way through the last bunch of brush, we found ourselves in the mouth of a mine.

My pied animal spooked when I tried to push her in after Owens's dun. I didn't blame the cuss much. There was something scary about that shaft. Not the fact that the beams looked ready to crumble in on you any minute. Not even the darkness that closed in blacker than sin after we'd left the meager light near the entrance. It was something else. Something an animal recognizes where a man can't. I've learned to trust in their judgment.

"No wonder the Douglas clan was hard to find," I said, more to make sure he was there than anything else. "What happened to the rest of her family? Didn't she have a brother named Natividad?"

"He's supposed to be in Mexico, trying to get help," said Owens. "A couple of her womenfolk have been seen down in the Chisos Mountains. That's my old pasture, and they have friends among the Mexicans in the back country. With the grapevine they've got down here, it wouldn't do much good for you to hunt them up. Word of your movements travels about as fast as you can, and the Chisos are just about as deadly as these mountains, if you don't know them."

"This mine is supposed to be over two hundred years old?"

"Simeon Santiago discovered it in Sixteen Eighty-One," he told me. "His engineer was an Englishman named Douglas. The shaft caved in and trapped Douglas and his wife and a bunch of *peones* in the valley. They lived there until Eighteen Ninety, cut off from the outside world."

"I know the story," I said. "And the Scorpion is supposed to be descended from this Douglas ranny."

"You sound skeptical," he said.

"It's possible," I told him.

"But not probable?" he said.

"You're a better judge of that than I am, being tied into all this so much," I told him.

"I've seen evidence."

"All right," I told him. "All I care about is Elgera Douglas, not her family history. Help me find her, and I'll even believe that Indian story about her being able to change from a woman into a real scorpion whenever she wants, if that'll please you."

He made a disgusted sound, and there was no more talk. I don't know how long it took us to stumble through that twisting, turning mine. He must have used up a pocketful of matches, trying to find our way back after we'd made a wrong turn. Finally we reached the other end. It was night by that time, and the moon was out. The shaft opened onto a hillside, and from the lip

81

we could look down into the Lost Santiago Valley.

It must have been five miles across to where the Dead Horses started building that purple, jagged wall again, and twice as far to transverse the length of the valley, with the mountains lifting up at either end to enclose it completely. There was water along the valley's floor, because there was a dark matte of trees making a strip a few hundred yards board, seeming to run the complete length of the floor. Owens got down and began to squat around on the ground.

"No fresh tracks coming out of the mine," he said finally.

"Let's take a look at the house, anyway," I suggested.

He shrugged, and his Porter creaked as he climbed on again. The house was at the bottom of the slope, and, as we approached, I could see how the top bar on one of the big cottonwood corrals had fallen down. There was a porch around front, formed by a line of poles supporting an overhanging roof thatched with Spanish dagger. This thatching had dried and fallen through to litter the tiled floor of the porch. Moonlight came through the gaps this left and spilled like pools of yellow honey across the brown husks of thatching and the faded red tiles. Owens grunted like a tired cow, getting off his dun again. He hesitated before the big oak door. It had been painted blue once. It's a Mexican superstition about the Virgin Mary, I guess. It must have been some homemade paint, from some vegetable dye, because it was peeling off. I could see Owens's big barrel swell with the breath he took before he turned the hammered silver knob, and shoved the door open. I couldn't help stiffening up a little.

I saw his hand drop to his holstered Bisley, before he stepped in. It smelled like rotting leather inside, and of

82

old, molding earth. Like a grave, I thought, and then almost cussed out loud at myself. I could hear him fumbling around in the dark. Light flared, and I saw it was from an old camphine lamp on a big oak center table. There was something ghostly about the tarnished Spanish helmet on the mantel of the fireplace.

"That's two hundred years old," he said.

"O.K., O.K.," I said. "You want to flip to see who waters the horses?"

"I'd rather do it," he said. "That creek is drying up, and most of it's so full of alkali it'd eat the guts out of our nags. You'd have a tough time locating the good holes." He went out and came back in a minute with our saddle rolls, setting his frying pan and coffee pot on the table. "There's some Arbuckle's and a little bacon in my roll."

Then he left again. I could hear the creak of leather as he got in the hull. I could hear one of the animals snort, and then the pad of their hoofs, fading, softly dying. I stood, staring at that helmet. Two hundred years . . . all right, maybe it *was* two hundred years old. I went to the table and unlashed his roll and got out the sack of coffee, and the greasy paper of bacon. Then I realized I'd have to wait until he got back with the filled canteens to make coffee. I went over to a pile of wood in the corner. It was rotten and crumbling, and must have been left here when the Scorpion high-tailed it. The hearth was of adobe, running the whole length of the wall at this end of the room, with holes along it at intervals for pot fires, and iron pothooks swinging out on either side of the main fireplace. I had a blaze started in one of the pot-fire holes when I heard Owens coming back. That creek must be nearer than it had looked. The pad of hoofs stopped outside.

"Kelly?"

It was soft, and husky, from out there. It was a woman's voice.

"Yeah," I said, after the moment it took me to recover, muffling my voice with my sleeve a little. There was a creak of saddle leather . . . the tap of high-heeled boots across the tiles . . . the dry shuffle of the same boots through some of the Spanish dagger that had fallen off the overhang.

"No," I said, "don't buy that trunk quite yet. You ain't going any place but in."

She had started to whirl away, with the first sight of me. But the Cloverleaf house gun in my hand kept her from doing it. The door made a perfect frame for her. I thought Cecile had been pretty, but she didn't hold a hog-fat candle to this filly.

Tall for a girl, taller than me in the spike heels of those basket-stamped peewees she wore. The Mexican *charro* pants I'd heard so much of, fitting just as tightly as they said, with red roses sewn down the seams. The white *camisa* for a shirt, fitting the same way, tightly in the right places, tucked into a crimson sash of Durango silk tied around her waist. And the hair like taffy, or gold, or I don't know what—why try to compare it, when it's so much just by itself? I was a mite surprised by the little whip dangling from her left wrist. Unless I'd missed a detail in previous descriptions, this fancy quirt was something new for *Señorita* Scorpion.

"If you're really a scorpion," I said, "come on in and bite me."

Her eyes flashed like a gun barrel, catching the sun. I moved my Cloverleaf a little to let her know I wasn't joking as much as it sounded, and she stepped on in.

"Lay that dewey down on the table," I told her, and

84

her fingers closed a little around the barrel of her Winchester, and then she stepped over to put it on the table. "Funny," I said. "I guess I've heard as much about that Army Colt you pack, and how good you are with it, as I've heard about your horse. And yet, according to the witnesses, this was the dewey you used on the senator, too. What's the conundrum?"

She ran her hands down her hips like she wished the Colt was there, and then her lips twisted. "Who are you?" she said, in a small, strained voice, harsh as mesquite scraping a saddle skirt.

"United States Marshal Powder Welles," I told her. "I've got a warrant there in my saddle roll. It's for the arrest of Elgera Douglas, alias *Señorita* Scorpion. Craziest alias I've ever heard. I served one on a jasper called himself Clarence the Cat once, but. . . ."

"Oh, shut up," she hissed at me, still standing stiff as a poker with those hands clawed against her legs. It struck me her eyes weren't right on me. They were looking over my shoulder. There was a loud pop, and I couldn't help jumping and whirling around. It was just a rotten chunk of wood, spitting its last as the fire ate it up. But by the time I'd seen that, it was too late. I was already whirling back as the crash came from the other direction. She'd knocked the lamp off the table, and there wasn't enough light left from that dying fire to put in the end of a coffin nail. I threw myself aside, figuring she'd go for that Winchester and was right. The room seemed to come apart at the seams with the sound of it. I saw the flash and heard the blue whistler go by me and on into the wall. My chivalry was worn thin, but I kept myself from firing at the flash, with an effort, and shouted at her from where I'd landed on my knees up against the wall after jumping aside that way.

85

"Honey, you'll be skylighted going through that door, and I swear I'll curl you up, if you try it."

I could hear her scratchy breathing from somewhere on the other side of the big room. The windows were shuttered tight, but moonlight made a yellow rectangle of that open door, and she must have realized how right I was, because I couldn't hear her moving. The moonlight didn't help me any more than that, although, way back where I was, it was still as dark as a dirty boot. Then she stopped breathing.

I could hear it, too, the sound of approaching horses, and I took the chance and hollered at him: "Chisos, don't come in. We got your gal corralled, and she's just as liable to send you to hell on a shutter as not."

"Elgera?" It came from Owens in a cracked way, out there, and then creaking leather as he swung off. "Elgera, are you in there?"

"Get him, Chisos," she said. "He's a marshal."

"No, Elgera." I could hear him coming toward the porch. "He's going to give you a chance. He knows there's something fishy about what's going on."

"What do you mean . . . a chance?" Her voice sounded thin.

"Give us the facts," I said. "Did you kill Bailes?"

"Think I'm a fool?"

"All right, we'll pass that up," I said. "Why did you kill him, then? What had he found out that would have spoiled your saddle?"

"Is that what you call giving me a chance?" she asked. "Answer any one of those questions, and I'd be putting my head in the noose. I won't admit killing him. I won't admit anything. Chisos, if you love me, get me out of here."

"Don't come in, Chisos," I said. "I want this

86

straightened out before you come in."

"Elgera, I tell you, he'll do to ride the river with," called Owens. "Won't you let us help you? You were seen by a dozen people when you killed Bailes. But you must have had a good reason. That's the only thing I can go on. What was Bailes doing? Was he mixed up with that mustang-running himself?"

"What have you found out working for T.S.A.?" she asked.

"I've got a relief man on that Butcherknife line camp who used to work for an affiliate of T.S.A. in Kansas," said Owens. "He broke horses for this affiliate till one stove him up, and T.S.A. pulled him down here on a job he could handle. This Kansas affiliate was one of the outfits the Army gave contracts to for broncos. The contract wouldn't let the affiliate put their own brand on the animals till they were broken. This buster says he saw more than one Mexican brand on them broomtails before he broke them."

"Is that the tie-in?" I asked her. "Kelly Striker's on T.S.A., and he managed the senator's election campaign in the old days. Was Bailes really the brains behind this border-hopping mustang outfit? If you had that good a reason for killing him, sugar, you might get out on extenuating circumstances."

"Don't be stupid . . . !"

"I'm only trying to see you get your deal from off the top, blondie," I said, riled a little now. Nobody likes to be called stupid, not even an old knothead like me. "Give us something to work with, will you? I can't see a smart gal like you pulling a trick like that without a good reason, any more than Chisos can. Who was that you asked for when you first rode up? Kelly? Kelly Striker? Why should he be here?"

87

"He wasn't here," she said. "Chisos, if you don't get me out, I'll do it myself. You're a fool for trusting any lawman like this."

"I'm coming in, Marshal," Owens said.

"Don't, Chisos, please," I called to him, but his boots tapped across the tiles, and his silhouette filled the door. I couldn't cut him down cold like that. Then the room began to rock again, with gunshots.

"Damn you, Marshal," I heard Owens shout, and he threw himself into the room from the doorway, until I heard his big body smash into the table.

"I didn't do it, Chisos," I hollered, rising from against the wall, and he must have heard me, because there was a heavy groan and a scraping sound, and then something like a herd of buffaloes smashed into me, and I went down under the table he had heaved my way.

"Get out, Elgera, get on out!" he shouted.

The table was turned completely over on me, and I was pinned beneath it from the waist down. It had knocked my house gun from my hand, so I couldn't even cut one at the girl as her silhouette appeared for a moment in the moonlit door. When I went to get out from beneath the furniture, I began to appreciate Owens's strength. It was like trying to move a house off me. There was a stumbling, shuffling sound, and another silhouette filled the doorway, blocking out light. Owens must have heard me trying to get from beneath the table, because it looked like he turned in again. About that time my legs came free.

I tried to stand up, but my legs had been mashed up a lot, and they wouldn't support me. I fell over toward Owens, and he must have thought I was coming for him. I heard the grunt he made, launching himself. I tried to get up again and meet it, but he struck me, and it felt just like that table again. I went to the floor beneath his hot, pounding weight with the noise of a running horse receding in my ears.

"So you'd give her a chance, would you?" panted Owens, and I thought the roof had fallen in on my face. I tried to roll free of him and get a grip on his wrist so he wouldn't hit again, but he spraddled his weight out over me and, rising up from the hips, that fist smashed into my face once more. I had gotten a hint of his terrible strength back there at Cecile's. Now as he clutched at my side with a hand, I felt like the whole kak was being cinched on.

I heard the small, muffled sounds of pain I made, jerking beside him. He hit at me again, and the dark and my struggles caused him to miss my face and catch my shoulder. It sent a ringing numbness down my arm. I caught his thick neck with my good hand, clawing, grasping. He tore my hand away, twisting my arm up. I heard a cracking noise, and a scream, and then realized it was me. Again that roof smashed down in my face. A light went on somewhere. At first, I thought it was the lamp. Then, in a little, small thought way down inside me, I realized there wasn't any light anywhere, really.

## IV

*THERE AIN'T NO HOSS THAT CAN'T BE THROWED. THERE ain't no man that can't be rode. If you're really a scorpion, come on in and bite me. What have you found out, working for T.S.A.? I've found a gal in Alpine pretty as a spotted dog under a red wagon. That won't do you no good. Her hair ain't dyed. It's auburn clear down to the roots. And somebody in Alpine would recognize her, even if she did dye her hair. Wouldn't*

89

*they? Don't ask me. I'm Kelly Striker. You're Kelly Striker . . . ?*

That's what brought me out of it, I guess, because I couldn't be Kelly Striker. He didn't have a broken arm. I lay there, feeling the hard-packed earth of the floor against my back and staring up at the herringbone fashion of willow shoots that lay across the *viga* posts which form the rafters in adobe houses. I lay there, wondering which hurt worse, my broken arm, or my slashed face. I didn't want to move, knowing both of them would hurt more when I did. I could see it was daylight outside now. Morning, because it was still a little cool. I'd been unconscious that long?

Finally I managed to roll over and crawl to the door. My mare was cropping at some curly brown mesquite grass downslope.

"Pie," I said, "will you come here," and the effort almost made those lights go out again. She just kept browsing. It hurt so I kept groaning with every spasmodic effort I made, crawling toward her. She lifted her head and that glass eye looked at me questioningly. *Damn you, after all we been through together, you just stand there and look like that.* "Come here." *Can't you see I need help? That Owens cuss thought he beat me to death! He'll see.* "Come here."

Finally I got to her. She shied a little, when I reached up for a stirrup leather. I don't know how long it took me to get in the saddle. I don't want to remember. I turned her upslope. It took us half the day to get through that cave. Maybe I passed out inside, or maybe it was just that dark. It was late afternoon when we reached the cañon on the other side. That fight through the thick brush choking the cut was the worst part, I guess. I lost count of how many times I was torn from the saddle. I

90

was glad for a horse like Pie then. Any other animal would have spooked and run away the first time I fell, with all that mesquite cracking and popping and me yelling like crazy.

I knew the old Comanche Trail came through Persimmon Gap in the Santiagos and lined down on this side of the Dead Horses to the Río Grande, and, if I could reach it, there was an outside chance I'd be picked up. It was night before I got free of Dead Man's Cañon. The next time I fell off my horse, I stayed off. Somewhere way off I could hear a coyote yammering. It began to get cold, and I started shivering. I couldn't stop. Maybe it was more reaction than chill. Then I passed out again.

Ⓥ Ⓥ Ⓥ Ⓥ Ⓥ

"*Los muertos no hablan.*"

"Speak English, will you? My cow-pen Spanish don't fit this poke."

"He said the dead don't speak, *señor*."

I looked up to see the two heads bending over me, one a big, fat, greasy pan almost lost in the shadow of a sombrero, the other a soft, tinted face with eyes as blue as the Virgin Mary color they put on their doors . . . and hair like taffy, or gold . . . or why try to compare it?— and I knew that I was unconscious.

*Carretas*, they call them, those big carts with solid wheels and cottonwood rails on the side. I could feel myself being lifted into it. The smell of fresh onions gagged me. I wondered how the smell could be so strong in a dream. Or maybe it wasn't a dream. But then, no human woman has a lap as soft as that. She had gotten in the cart with me and had sat down so her legs

91

formed a pillow for my head. I could even feel the red suede of her *charro* pants.

"Oh, look at his face," she said in a soft, horrified way.

Her voice at the house had been thin and scratchy. It was rich and full now, like running Durango silk through your hands. I opened my eyes. Her mouth was different, too, somehow—the lips riper and softer. Her whole face seemed softer. I wondered if she still wore that whip.

"Women are crazy critters," I muttered.

Her laugh was small, cutting off short, but it held something wild that clutched at me. "You're all right," she said, "as long as you can gripe like that. What happened to you?"

"Most of it happened after you left. Chisos. . . ."

"Chisos!"

"Yeah," I said.

"Oh, the fool, the fool," she murmured in a soft, husky way.

"No," I told her, "I was the fool. But now I've got you, and you're coming back with me."

She laughed again. "Yes," she said, "you've got me, but, before I go anywhere with you, you'd better get patched up a little. We're going to Avarillo's at Boquillos."

Well, all right, I thought, maybe we had better, because I didn't want to take my head off that soft lap just yet anyway, and I sort of snuggled back, and then the whole thing cut its picket pin and drifted off.

Ⓥ Ⓥ Ⓥ Ⓥ Ⓥ

"*Señor*, I have seen plenty of rawhide in my time, and

92

there are *compadres* of mine who swear on the Virgin's name that it wears better than iron, but I never saw a man made from it before. I have some horseshoe nails out in the back, and I have been discussing with myself whether you would thrive more on them than you would on this baby food my great, fat aunt insists will cure you."

I wasn't in the cart any more. I was in another adobe room, with slots for windows and hard-packed earth for a floor. The bed was made of hand-hewn oak slabs pegged together, and the covers of dirty, red wool smelled like goats had been sleeping in them. The man who wanted to feed me horseshoe nails stood beside the bed with a clay platter of some steaming hog tripe.

I've seen steers rolling in so much tallow they couldn't walk, but this jasper made them look like skin and bones. He had so many chins there was no telling where his jaw ended and his neck began. The sweat ran like grease from the creases. He had on a broad black belt, buckled up like he was trying to hold in some of the gut that slopped over it in great rolls that looked like white sausages in his thin silk shirt with the flowing sleeves. His eyes were like a bloodhound that I had seen once, big and sad and bloodshot, with that liquid look that makes you think they're going to spill out and run down his cheeks any minute. I'd worked long enough on this case, now, to know most of the people mixed up with the Scorpion, and there was no missing the gate in this corral.

"Ignacio Juan y Felipe del Amole Avarillo," I said.

"*Sí*, mining engineer *extraordinario*, archeologist *magnífico*, consultant on affairs of the heart, or whatever else you happen to require at the moment," he chuckled. "You are well informed, Marshal Welles."

93

"Where's the Scorpion?" I asked.

He raised fat eyebrows. "They have a saying down here, Marshal. *¿Quién sabe?* Who knows?"

"She brought me here."

"A peon and his wife brought you here," said Avarillo. "They found you on the Comanche Trail in this sad condition."

"Then I *was* dreaming," I said.

"*Sí*," he said. "Now try to get down some of this *pinole con leche*. And after that, we will dress your face again. My aunt has soaked the seeds of Guadalupina vine in mescal for three days. It will not make you handsome again, but it will heal the wounds."

"I wasn't handsome to begin with," I said. "How about that hog tripe? I'm hungry."

"Not hog tripe, *señor*, please," chuckled Avarillo. "It is parched corn fluff and milk."

Whatever it was, I ate it. Then his big, fat aunt came in with this stuff soaked in mescal juice. She made Avarillo look like a ganted dogie. If his cheeks were so fat they almost hid his eyes, I couldn't even see her eyes. She kept tugging at her pale-blue satin shawl and chuckling, and a different part of her body quivered every time she chuckled. It got on my nerves, somehow. Then, once, I caught a glimpse of her eyes, behind all that doughy fat. They weren't chuckling.

"Where's my dewey?" I said.

"Please, *señor*, I have not finished dressing your face. Your what?"

"My cutter, my lead chucker, my hogleg . . . ?"

"Ah, he means his gun, my big, fat *tía*," grinned Avarillo.

"In a safe place, *señor*," she told me.

"Yeah?" I started to get up, but his big, fat aunt

94

caught me by the shoulders.

"Please, Marshal Welles," objected Avarillo. "You are in no condition to excite yourself. Perhaps I should introduce you to Moro. He is my . . . ah . . . man, you might say. He is a Quill, a pure-blooded Indian of Mexico, and he is a very good card player. Come in, Moro."

Moro came in. I've seen a few Quills. There's something different about them you don't get in an Indian like a Comanche, or an Apache. It's like the difference between an oily bronco with a glass eye that's so full of the hokey-pokey he's always jumping around and you're on your guard every second, and a big fool with a streak of Quarter in him, maybe, who just sulks along till you've quit watching him, and then up and flips the kak. That was Moro. His eyes might as well have not been there for all they told. His mouth looked like somebody had cut a slit in his face with the blade of the big Arkansas toothpick he carried stuck nakedly through the rawhide dally holding up his *chivarras*.

"*¿Chusa?*" he said, shuffling a pack of greasy, horsehide cards through fingers like big Fifty barrels.

"Poker's my game," I told him, "stud at that. I won't be here long enough to sit through a hand, anyway, Charlie."

"Moro," said Avarillo. "And I think you will be here, *señor*."

"When you took my wallet," I said, "did you happen to notice the U. S. marshal's badge pinned to the flap?"

"I respect the United States government, *señor*, more than you seem to think," grinned Avarillo. "But if it ever came to pass that they questioned my respect, all I would have to do is step across the river, and that is all

95

they could continue to do . . . question, if you see what I mean."

"¿*Chusa?*" repeated Moro.

"Hell," I said.

## V

IT WAS HOT DOWN THERE ON THE BORDER. I ATE A LOT and slept a lot, and I must have gained some weight, because my Levi's started getting tight around the waist. I felt like a hog, getting fattened for the killing. Moro stayed in the room most of the time, trying to teach me that *chusa*, but my cow-pen Spanish didn't help much, and the only word he knew in English wouldn't bear repeating in polite society.

After about the first week they let me up, figuring, no doubt, I couldn't cause too much trouble with that cracked wing. Avarillo ran the local saloon in town. They called it a *cantina*. My room was at the back, and it opened directly onto the *cantina* itself, which was no more than a couple of round tables to drink at and a row of barrels at the back set upon a wooden rack so Avarillo could operate the bung-starters.

Avarillo walked down the row of barrels, thumping each one as he spoke. "Mescal, Marshal! It will make a cock of a capon, a bull of a steer, a stallion of a gelding. Tequila? The kick of a mule is a love tap. Pulque? One drink and a kitten thinks he is a *tigre*."

"I'll take the bull-maker," I told him. "I need a little vinegar in my roan."

He poured me a big shot in a clay cup, nodding his head toward the outer door. There was a brush arbor to one side, and we sat at the table beneath that. Moro stood against one of the supports, idly shuffling his

96

horsehide cards. The town wasn't much more than this *cantina* and a bunch of mud houses hung on the outside with the same scarlet *ristras* of chili you see at old Haymarket Plaza in San Antonio. We could look across the narrow gorge of the Río Grande into Mexico.

"Boquillos is a corruption *boquilla* which means the little mouthpiece you find on a flute," Avarillo told me. "It came about because of the narrowness of the gorge here, no doubt."

"When you going to kill the hog?" I said.

Those eyebrows raised. "*¿Que?*"

"Back in Webb County we always fattened our bacon before the slaughter," I said.

Suddenly he began to chuckle, leaning forward and looking up into my face. "Don't I fit the role of a benevolent host, Marshal?"

"About as well as a dun trying to look like an albino," I said.

His chuckle spread over his whole body, in waves, and he peered closer. "You know, Marshal, my big, fat *tía* . . . she thinks you are so quaint, with your cynical colloquialisms. I imagine it amuses many people . . . doesn't it? . . . so that they overlook what lies behind it. I would not like to be Chisos Owens, right now. In his place, I would have rather killed you, than beaten you like that and left you alive. Perhaps Chisos does not realize it. Perspicacity is not one of his attributes. Perhaps not many people realize it, but I have always prided myself on my judge of character. I would hate to have you on my trail, Marshal." He leaned back, taking a deep breath. "We are not fattening you for the kill, Marshal. You may leave whenever you wish, my friend. No . . . ? *Sí.*"

"The Scorpion's far enough away to be out of my

97

reach . . . in other words?"

He began to chuckle again, throwing his fat, brown hands up and shrugging. "A man's most secret thought is not safe with you around, is . . . ?" It was like somebody had noosed a California collar up tight suddenly. He almost choked on the words. Then he stood up. "We have had our appetizer. Shall we repair to the festive board now?"

But I had seen that glance, past me. I got up and made to approach Moro, still leaning against the post. My good right arm was toward him as I passed, and he had just started to lean his weight forward away from the post when I did it, so casually he didn't know what happened till I had that blade out of his belt.

"I never repaired anything but a broken pack-saddle," I said. "I don't think I'll start treating my victuals that way so late in life. Instead, let's you and me just move around the corner, Moro, while Ignacio here meets whoever's coming up the trail from the cañon. Make a wrong move, and I'll cut out your brisket with this Arkansas toothpick."

"It is not a toothpick, *señor*," Moro told me, staring past us with a twisted face. "It is a *belduque*, used by the blood-drinkers of the *cordillera*."

"Whatever it is, act natural, or you'll have some more blood to drink," I told him. "Git, now, you black Injun."

I could feel Moro twitching, with that point in his gizzard. He walked around the corner like the ground was covered with bantam eggs he didn't want to break. Avarillo stood beneath the arbor, wringing his hands and cussing under his breath in Spanish. In a minute, a jasper bulged into view at the lower end of town, coming up a trail that looked like it started at the bottom of the cañon. He was over six feet tall, gaunt without

98

being skinny, something reckless about his slouch in the saddle. He had on a pair of old bullhide chaps, scarred and ripped with recent brush-riding, and his John B. Stetson had the Texas crease you can spot a mile away. The three-quarter rig was so sweaty even its creak was soggy as he swung off.

"Seen her?" he asked.

"No, no," said Avarillo, wringing his hands.

I could see the man's eyes now. Red-rimmed and grim, stabbing at Avarillo like nails pinning up a reward dodger. "She was up north of Alpine last Monday," he said in a hoarse, driven way. "Busted up a mustang drive. When it was over, the horses were scattered over all of Brewster County. Half of them had Mexican brands on. Wouldn't have been known, if she hadn't scattered them that way...."

Avarillo must have been making signs with those elevator eyebrows, because the man stopped suddenly, staring at the fat Mexican. I decided it was about time to intrude. I made my own signals with the point of that knife, and Moro reacted, moving around the corner.

"Leave your hands off your hardware, Sheriff Hagar," I told him. "I can cut both your ears off with one throw of this Arkansas toothpick."

"*Belduque, por favor*," groaned Moro.

"Or should I say ex-Sheriff Hagar," I told the newcomer. "Take both your deweys out and drop them on the ground, and don't try to pull no Curly Bill spin, or I'll curl *your* bill."

He gripped the ivory handles of his Peacemakers without putting his index fingers through the trigger guards, and eased them out. There was just a fraction's hesitation. I let my wrist twitch so the sunlight ran along the knife blade. The Peacemakers made dull thuds.

99

"Step away," I told him, and then went over and picked them up, stuffing them in my belt. Then, casual-like, I flipped the knife at one of the cottonwood supports holding up the arbor. It was at the other end, some ten feet away, a thin pole at that. Avarillo looked at the blade, quivering a little in the cottonwood. Then he looked at Johnny Hagar.

"Don't you look good," he chuckled, "still in your ears?"

"How do you know the Scorpion was up north of Alpine last Monday?" I asked Johnny Hagar.

His face was turned gray with dust, and sweat had made two glistening grooves from his nostrils to the corners of his thin, closed mouth.

I let my good hand move a little closer to one of the Peacemakers. "I could *shoot* your ears off just as well,"

He drew in a thin breath. "A dozen people saw her. A couple of big ranchers . . . the station agent at Sanderson . . . Spanish Jack."

"What was Jack doing there?" I said.

Hagar shrugged. "He was called in after it happened . . . cut her sign south of Alpine . . . lost her around Butcherknife."

Avarillo must have seen the expression on my face, and it must have been going around in his mind for some time now. "Just what was the fight between you and Chisos Owens about, Marshal?"

"We had found Elgera Douglas at the Lost Santiago," I said. "He was trying to keep me from taking her back to Alpine."

Just before a norther hits sometimes, it gets as quiet as that. I don't think they were even breathing. Finally Hagar let out a disgusted breath.

"That's impossible. She couldn't have made it from

100

Alpine to the Santiago in the same day. Not even on her palomino."

"She was there," I said.

"And she was north of Alpine," he said. "Beyond any doubt."

"One of us is lying," I said.

"There is a dead man who once called Sheriff Hagar a liar," smiled Avarillo.

"I hope he doesn't get too tetchy on that point of honor now," I said. "Seeing as how I've got the hardware."

"We seem to have reached an impasse," said Avarillo.

"If you mean, we're up against a fence, not necessarily," I said. "Finding the Scorpion might clear up this little discrepancy, as well as a few others. You seem to have been working hard trying to locate her too, Hagar. Why is that?"

"I don't think she murdered Bailes."

"That was witnessed," I said.

"She must have had a good reason, then," he said.

"You change horses pretty quick," I said. "Is yours a reason that would stand up in a court of law?"

He shook his head from side to side like a bull with blowflies. "I don't know, but. . . ."

"I think you're in the same wagon Chisos Owens was," I said. "You're in love with the gal, and you want to ride her trail, no matter what she does. A man that dizzy over a filly ought to be willing to make a deal."

"What kind of deal?"

"Be careful, Johnny," said Avarillo.

"I took it for granted, to begin with, that Chisos Owens knew where the Scorpion was," I said. "But I don't think he'd deliberately lead a lawman onto her,

101

the way things happened. So now, I'm taking it for granted you don't know where she is. She seems snubbed in pretty tight to this mustang-running gang. I think maybe once we find out their secrets, we'll find hers. Nobody has been able to find where they cross the border. You probably know more about this section of the Río than anybody, Ignacio, from what I hear of you. How about it?"

He shrugged his fat shoulders. "The buzzard leaves no tracks in the sky."

"And a blind bronco also tears up a lot of brush on his way to the water hole," I said, "if you go in for sayings. And that's just what I'd be, wandering around down here. I'd tear up a helluva lot of chaparral before I found the sink. You can let me go on alone, if you want, but there's no telling what I'd bump into, or turn up. Wouldn't you rather be there when it happened, than not?"

Avarillo looked at Hagar. "He is right, Johnny. With a man like the marshal, it is sometimes better to help him than let him run around loose."

"If you two aren't mixed up in this mustang-running yourselves, and know where they're crossing, I can't see what you'd have against showing me," I told them.

"Good," said Hagar, "but get this, Marshal. If we find the Scorpion, and you try to take her in, there isn't anything I won't do to stop you, even if I have to kill you."

## VI

I'D THOUGHT THAT RIDE INTO THE SANTIAGO HAD BEEN through the worst badlands this side of the misty beyond, but they were blueroot pastures from a

102

mortgaged cowman's dream compared with what Avarillo and Hagar dragged me into. It all seemed connected with death, somehow, and that didn't help. Below Boquillos was Dead Man's Turn, where some grissel-heel had been shot on a high ride. Beyond that was the old Smuggler's Trail with a big stone tower overlooking it which they called Murderer's Haunt because some blue bellies had been starved to death there during the War Between The States. And then on into the Dead Horse Mountains again.

"From Alpine on down," Avarillo told me, "the Santiagos and the Dead Horses make a spine of impassable mountains with Rosillos Basin on their west side, and Maravillas on their east. The Smuggler's Trail crosses the Río just east of Boquillos, and then either turns up or down, east or west. The rangers know that this ancient trail is being used by the mustang-runners, but they always turn either east or west on this side of the river, looking for them to take either the Rosillos Basin north, or the Maravillas. To their knowledge, there is no known way through the Dead Horses. It would be certain death. But that is only to their knowledge."

"And to *your* knowledge, there's a trail striking due north through the Dead Horses into the Santiago Valley," I said. "Once in the valley, they've got that creek to carry them through."

He was sitting on an Arizona nightingale that was packing as much tallow as he was, the animal rigged out with an old Mother Hubbard saddle and a spade bit with shanks as long as shovel handles. *You'd need that much leverage*, I thought, *to stop that iron-mouthed knothead*.

"Your perspicacity constantly amazes me, Marshal," he said.

103

"Simple geography," I said. "And I suppose you aren't the only one who knows this trail. Since it goes right into the Scorpion's home pasture, I suspect she knows of it."

The Mother Hubbard creaked like a rusty gate, as he leaned his weight toward me, looking sorry as grease. "You think she is running the mustangs?"

"What else does it add up to?"

"Perhaps we had better not take you through," he said.

"I could do it alone, and, if the Scorpion winds up on the end of this one, she'll find herself in Alpine faster'n a water bucket down a go-devil," I told him.

"Oddly enough," he said, "I think you could. No one else has, but I think you could. That is why we shall go on, if you wish."

I wished. Maybe I was sorry for it afterward. No trees. No brush. Not even those rings of stones you find out in the Rosillos, blackened on the inside where some Comanches had roasted *sotol* stalks maybe a hundred years before. Just sand and rocks and creosote and sun. Pie had taken on some tallow with Avarillo's grain, but I could see it lather up and drip off her, pound by pound.

There ain't no hoss that cain't be rode.
There ain't no man that cain't be throwed.

"*Señor*, must you add to our misery?"

"Oh, go ahead and let him sing, Avarillo, I kind of like it." Hagar grinned as he said it. I'd heard about that grin, too, and how nothing short of the devil could wipe it off, and maybe not even him. I began to appreciate it farther on, when I couldn't even sing. That was when we found the first dead mustang.

104

We had turned north, away from the Río Grande into those Dead Horses. I don't know how many miles it was up off the river. I'd lost count. I know we'd started at daybreak, and it was now late afternoon. Hagar was leading us on his apron-faced horse, and it shied suddenly in a weary, reluctant way. I saw it, then, lying beyond some creosote bushes, and had to haul up the ribbons on my own piebald to keep her from spooking. The buzzards had been at the carcass, but the brand was still evident on the flea-bitten hide.

"*El Reja*," said Avarillo. "That is quite a big outfit in Mexico."

"Looks like it's been dead a long time," I remarked. "We're not on a fresh trail."

"No?" murmured Avarillo. The way he said it made me look at him. But he'd already turned that mule away and started on up the cut.

We lined deeper into the Dead Horses, stark peaks all around us. Then the sun went down, and it was darker than the inside of a ramrod's yannigan bag. Finally the moon came up as fat and yellow as a Webb County pumpkin, and its light turned the country into the kind of a picture a ranny sees after painting his nose all night. Sometimes the hogbacks turned red as the tops of a kid's Hyers; next they might be as green as wheatgrass in spring with big, purple rocks poking out like post-oak bumps on a brush popper's legs.

"All right," said Johnny Hagar abruptly, and swung down off his dun. We'd been traveling across shaley ground, but now we had struck a strip of sand, and it was all churned up like a band of stuff had been run through here. There were droppings, too. Hagar toed some. "Fresh enough," he said. "Push a little, and we might tie into them."

105

Pie was so played out I had to keep giving her the boot. We crossed a saddle between two peaks and on the opposite slope saw the haze, swimming atop the next row of hills. We flagged our kites at a hard gallop down the slope and up the next. Just before the ridge, Hagar stepped off his horse and moved to the top on foot, squatting down when he reached it, to keep from being skylighted.

"Sure enough," he said. "Big bunch of them, fogging through that next valley. Looks like a full band of riders. . . ."

Maybe it was in the way he stopped. He could have ended it there, all right. But his voice sounded like a tight dally snipped off suddenly. His whole lean body stiffened, and he started to turn toward us, still squatted down like that, then wheeled back, and finally, rising at the same time, turned back toward us.

"Don't do it, Hagar," I said. "Is she down there?"

No telling what makes a man hesitate in a moment like that. Whatever it was, it gave me the chance to thwart his original intention. He had the look of going for his guns, although his hands did not actually move. I can't figure him backing down on a draw-out, even though in his moment of hesitation his glance was pinned on my own hand, close enough to that Cloverleaf in my belt. At any rate, I had already booted my horse up, and by the time he went into his final move, faced toward me, I was close enough to ram my horse in against him, knocking him off balance.

"Marshal, I told you . . . ," he gasped, grabbing for my bridle.

But I was on the crest, then, and could see down into the next valley. A bunch of mustangs was being run northward beneath a dirty-brown mist of their own dust.

106

There were two riders dragging, one on swing, and one on point. I couldn't make out what color their horses were exactly. But there's one color you can't miss, even under those conditions. It's that pale gold tint of a true palomino, set off by the pure white mane and tail. And there it was, outriding, on the opposite slope, and the rider had hair as blonde as the horse's.

Hagar had the shank of my bit in one hand now, and his tug caused Pie to whinny and rear up. I necked hard to the right, swinging the animal around into him by its rump, and freeing one foot from the stirrup at the same time. My boot caught him under the chin. He made a sound like a roped dogie when it hits the ground, and the sudden release of his hold on my bit caused Pie to plunge forward. Hagar was falling over backward, and I had swung out my stirrups to kick the horse on over the hill, when Avarillo's voice came from behind me, soft and bland as hog fat dripping down a candle.

"Not quite now, Marshal, if you please."

Any other man, I might have gone on and kicked Pie over the hill. But there was something in his voice that made me turn around, still holding my feet out that way. I don't know where he'd gotten the stingy gun. It was a little four-barreled Krider pepperbox almost hidden in his fat hand, but at this range it would be deadly.

"I'm going on over, Avarillo," I told him. "She's down there, and I'm going to nail her this time, and nobody is stopping me. If you want to open my back door, go ahead."

I turned my back on him. I didn't make the mistake of hustling over the crest. I dropped my feet in easy, heeling Pie into a deliberate walk. Hagar lay on the ground, watching in an unbelieving daze. Then I was over the top and going down the other side.

Once beneath the crest I pushed Pie into a gallop down the steep talus, praying for the sure feet she'd shown so many times before, giving her a free bit and letting her slide, when she wanted. I was right on the flank of the band and quartered in, meaning to drop behind the drag riders and pick up the girl on the other side. But I didn't use enough cover, I guess. They must have caught sight of me coming down. Somebody started gun racket.

I couldn't hear any of those blue whistlers, whining my way, or see them kicking up dirt around me, but the gunshots came from down there somewhere. It was a case of hive right on in or duck, and I wanted that girl too much to turn my tail.

"Git on there, you piebald cousin to a rat-tailed ridge runner," I howled at Pie, and she really lined out under that, because she knows I never yell at her unless I really want to shovel on the coal. The gunshots mingled now with the sound of running horses to deafen me, and the dust billowed up to gag me, and I raced around the drag end of that band of pepper-gut broncos. A horsebacker bulged out of the blinding dust ahead. He was turned the other way in the saddle with his Winchester, and it surprised me. He jerked around my way, when he saw me coming, looking as surprised as I was, and pulled his rifle over the saddle bows.

I cut loose with my Cloverleaf, shooting at his horse. I saw his hat twitch off, and that's how accurate you can be on a running animal with a six-iron. His Winchester made its bid then. I saw it buck across his saddle bows and saw it reach out with that red finger. I could feel Pie jerk against my legs. *Damn you, if you've dusted my horse*, I thought, and squeezed my trigger again, kicking my feet free of the stirrups at the same time. Pie went

108

head over heels, and I threw myself clear, trying to roll it off.

But the ground was rocky, and my broken arm caught it. I heard myself bawl like a roped heifer, and then went flopping off across rocks as sharp as a razorback hog, howling and grunting before coming to a stop against a boulder.

I lay there a minute, spinning like a trick roper's Blocker loop. I could hear somebody groaning. It was I. When I realized that, I knew I was beginning to come out of it. My busted wing hurt even worse than the first time it had been snapped. The thunder of running horses had faded into the distance, and the gunshots were farther off, too, not coming so hot and heavy now. Then I began to hear that other sound. It was like something scraping over rocks. It *was* something scraping over rocks.

"Jerry?" called someone. "Was that you going down?"

I had cover on one side from the boulder. I could see my Cloverleaf, lying out in the open where I'd dropped it. I had to make a quick decision, and decided I'd rather checkout, making some kind of bid, than just sit here and wait for them to rake the pot in. I rolled over on my belly and began snaking toward my iron. I was within a couple of feet of it, when that scraping sound stopped, and it was the soft, gritty noise of boots stepping into sand. My fingers were an inch away from that Cloverleaf-shaped cylinder on my Colt house gun, when he spoke from behind.

"Don't do that quite yet, Marshal. I want to enjoy this a while before I send you to hell on that shutter you unhinged for yourself back at Cecile's."

I stayed in that position a minute, or a year, I don't

109

know. Then I twisted my head around, with my hand still pawed out that way, so I could see him. I had already recognized his voice, of course.

"Well, Bryce," I said, "light down and give your horse a rest."

There was a small, puckered scar in the flesh of his cheek, like someone had punctured it with something, and he wore a black patch over one eye. He passed the palm of his free hand over that side of his face, without actually touching it, and his lips pulled away from his teeth in a flat grin.

"I've been waiting for this, Marshal," he said. "You don't know how long I've been waiting for this. You don't know how I've thought and dreamed and planned this moment. I never hoped to have the drop on you, of course. I thought it would have to be flip-cock and shoot, and all the pleasure would have to be after you was dead. This is so much better.

"Start squirming, Marshal. I'm not going to kill you right off. I'm going to shoot you in the legs, so you can't move away, and then in the belly. That will take a long time. Hours . . . maybe even a day or so. With your tripe leaking out the hole, Marshal, and the sun coming up and burning you like a match roasting a fly. Ain't you going to beg, Marshal? If you beg a little, maybe I'll let you off easy."

I began to sweat. I couldn't help that. I didn't figure he'd be so nice as to put out my bull's-eye quick, even if I did squall. The only thing I could hope would end it fast was if I took a quick grab for my gun and made him take a snap shot. He couldn't be as certain that way, and there was an outside chance it might snuff my candle then. Two pair against a straight, but there weren't any more draws left in this game for me. My whole body

110

stiffened. He must have seen it. He cocked his Forty-Four.

I decided I might as well step in the kak, now as any time, and reached out for my Cloverleaf. I never heard a gun go off louder. My whole body jerked so tightly I cried out with the shock it sent through me. But somehow I could still get my fingers around the walnut grips of my own gun, and I turned over on my back with it in my hand.

Bryce Wylie was standing on his toes. He was looking down at them. Even his gun was pointed at his toes. There was a sick look on his face. Then, slowly, still hanging there like he was in a California collar, his left hand reached across and spread out over his belly. His gun dropped out of his right hand, and he pitched over on his face.

As I lay there, staring at him, it came to me that I felt no pain, that it was not Wylie who had shot at all. I rolled over on my belly and helped myself onto my knees with my good hand.

"Well," I said, "if you aren't the shootin'est gal I've ever seen."

"You've got a lot of sand in your own craw, Marshal," the Scorpion said, coldly blowing the smoke from the end of the big Army Colt she held and stuffing it back into the holster.

Her hair shone like wet gold. Her bottom lip was ripe as 'possum berries in the spring, and the shadow beneath it made her look like she was pouting. And now was the time to wear a whip, but she didn't have one.

"Saving my life that way sort of complicates matters," I told her. "I really meant it when I said I was going to take you in, Elgera."

It's funny, the shine blue eyes get in that way.

111

"Before you even heard my side of the story?"

"I'm listening."

"What would that behind you indicate?" she said.

"That I was cussed lucky you came along just then."

"Not lucky. I saw what happened from the other slope. But I don't mean that. Doesn't Wylie and Jerry Hammer's connection in this mean anything to you?"

"They're Spanish Jack's men," I said.

"And Jack is Kelly Striker's man," she said.

"You mean the T.S.A.?" I asked her.

"You're a government man," she said. "Couldn't you have a government auditor go over their books?"

"They're shaky?"

"It would be my bet that T.S.A. is in as much red ink as they are blood," she told me. "Why should a big corporation like that contract to handle my cattle for the courts till this thing is cleared up? What they make off that won't be chicken feed compared with what they get handling beef they can drive to market."

"Maybe you're working for Striker, too," I said. "So when Bailes finds out T.S.A. is pulling a fast one, he has to be eliminated, and Striker picks you for the job."

"That's not very logical," she said, and I could see the flush beginning to tint her face that colored her words. "Kelly Striker has been bucking me in Brewster County for years."

"It's not very logical that you would shoot Chisos Owens back at the Santiago and then save my life, either," I said.

"Chisos!" Now I could see the color seep out of her face. She bent toward me, letting it out in a heavy breath. "Where! Where is he, Welles?"

"You ought to know better than I," I told her. "When I came around back in your house, he was gone, too. I

112

figured he'd taken out after you."

"After me? What are you talking about?"

"At the Santiago," I said. "That Monday. What had you done . . . just run another band of these pepper-guts through?"

That buttermilk horse of hers stood a few feet behind her, and she began to back toward it. Her eyes were shining slits in her face. "You're trying to forefoot me. I wasn't at the Santiago on any Monday since Bailes was killed. Chisos isn't shot."

"You ought to know," I said. "But all that blood on the floor at Santiago wasn't mine. I think you gut-shot him good, and he's either holed up somewhere or dead . . . somewhere."

"It's the same thing that happened in Alpine," she muttered.

"What happened in Alpine?" I said.

"I wasn't there."

"You weren't there when?"

"Marshal. . . ." She was bent toward me now, hands closing into fists. "Tell me the truth. Chisos isn't shot."

"I think he was," I said. "A blind greener couldn't have missed, the way he was skylighted in that door."

"Where is he?" she said.

"I don't know, Elgera," I said.

She started backing toward her horse again. I got the idea it wasn't what she had meant to do at first.

"Don't spook now," I told her. "Chisos's not here to throw you a clothesline, and I'm not losing you this time, Elgera. I try to remember what my ma taught me about being a gentleman, but I swear I'll forget every word she said . . . *Elgera!*"

She had whirled to that horse. I had never seen such a mount. The Mexicans teach their animals to whirl

113

outward, but this buttermilk nag spun toward the girl as she jumped into the air. Her left toe caught the stirrup, and the inward pinwheel of that animal slapped her into the saddle faster than I could follow. She drove the palomino right at me. But I was all horns and rattles now, I was so mad, and, instead of jumping out of the way, I let that pale, writhing chest hit me. It knocked me aside, but I was still in close enough to grab her leg as it went past me, and that kept me from falling.

The palomino wasn't in its full gallop yet, and my weight, tugging on the animal, pulled it down. Shouting something, the Scorpion tried to kick free, but I slid my grip on up her leg till I had my hand hooked in that Durango sash around her waist.

With the horse still going forward, the force of it pulled her back. She lost balance and came out of the saddle and on top of me. The fall stunned me. She kicked free and rolled off, trying to gain her feet at the same time. I rolled after her, with my left wing still out of commission. For just an instant we were face to face, still on the ground. My right arm was on the upper side, and I snaked it out and grabbed her left wrist, twisting her left arm around behind her in a hammerlock.

I was right up against her, with her breath hot in my face, so close I could see the little devils dancing in her eyes. She made another violent attempt to break free. I shoved that twisted arm farther up her back. She gasped with the pain and twisted around, shoving herself hard up against me to ease the pressure.

"All right," she panted in a final, despairing defeat, "all right."

"It better be," I said, without relaxing my hold. "Now are you going to be a good girl, or am I going to have to take you back to Alpine trussed in a lariat?"

114

"I'll be a good girl, Marshal," she breathed scathingly, facing away from me now. "I'll be a very good girl."

Maybe it was the husky emphasis she put on the last words. Maybe it was that heat in her voice. I don't know, but it struck me for the first time how tightly she was up against me, her backside pressed against my groin. I'd thought about her a lot before now, of course. A man couldn't help thinking about a thing like that on a case like this . . . from the beginning, from the very first story . . . a woman they called *Señorita* Scorpion, and then through all the other stories . . . and coming up against men like Chisos Owens and Johnny Hagar, ready to die just for another look at her . . . and then seeing her that first time at the Santiago, and thinking about it after that. But I didn't think about her now, and that was funny, after it had been on my mind so long . . . about her. Nothing at all was in my mind now. I didn't have any consciousness of what I was doing until she turned around again, slowly, as I let go of her arm. Then I felt the ripe, soft richness of her lips against my own.

I never will know how long it lasted. Finally it was I who pulled away. She stood there, taking slow, deep breaths, staring at me. Her eyes weren't half-closed in that sleepy way any more. They were staring at me in a strange, wide surprise.

"Somehow," she said in a husky whisper, "I hadn't thought of you . . . like that."

"I'd thought of you," I said. I could hardly get it out, my throat was so drawn up. "I've got no right . . . you're my prisoner . . . and I've got to take you in . . . and they'll probably hang you. But I can't help it."

The focus of her eyes changed for a second, not seeming to be on my face now. Then the expression on

115

her face changed, too.

"Powder?" she said in that husky way, and brought her lips in again.

I took it. Then I felt the stiffening of her whole body against me. Her arms slid along my sides and hooked around behind me, pulling me in. I tried to jerk my head back and get free of that grip, but I'd got the gate open too late. The whole State of Texas hit me on the back of my skull, and my head exploded and scattered pieces all over Mexico, and the Dead Horses opened up and swallowed me.

## VII

*I'VE BEEN WAITING FOR THIS A LONG TIME, MARSHAL . . . Chisos shot? . . . I tell you I wasn't at the Santiago. I'm going to shoot you in the legs, and then in the belly . . . ain't you going to beg, Marshal? So long since I held a woman. Somehow, I hadn't thought of you . . . like that.*

"If you don't stop talking so deliriously, Marshal," said Ignacio Juan y Felipe del Amole Avarillo, "you will not only reveal the details of your love life, but all the secrets of the United States government as well."

I opened my eyes to see him sitting cross-legged beside me, puffing calmly on a cheroot, his Arizona nightingale cropping at creosote behind him. It was daylight. I really doze a long time when they snuff my bull's-eye. Then I saw another animal working over the creosote beyond Avarillo's.

"Pie," I said, starting to raise up, and that was about as far as I got, before the back of my head seemed to split open.

He pushed me back down with a fat hand. "I thought the man with the Winchester had shot your horse, too,

116

when I saw you go down from where I was on the hill. But evidently the animal only stumbled in that rough ground."

I rubbed the back of my head. "Hagar?"

"It was Hagar who hit you from behind," said Avarillo. "Then he and the girl headed northward. My mule cannot keep up with that palomino of hers when she pushes it. Or perhaps even my dubious scruples would not allow me to leave you here to die."

I got up finally, trying not to cuss out loud. Once was bad enough. But twice, like this, struck a man's pride. Then my eye fell on Bryce Wylie's body, over by the boulder. It didn't seem to bother Avarillo.

"I got an idea from the gal, if nothing else," I said. "I can't figure Wylie and Hammer running these mustangs on their own. If Spanish Jack is behind this border-hopping, that leaves two possibilities. Either he's working for himself and double-crossing Striker, or he's working for Striker."

"And if he's working for Striker, that would bring in T.S.A.," said Avarillo.

"Chisos said something about an affiliate of T.S.A. in Kansas handling a lot of these Mexican broncos," I muttered. Then I lifted my head a little. "I wonder what Striker's reaction would be, if we showed up in Alpine with Bryce Wylie's body?"

Ⓥ Ⓥ Ⓥ Ⓥ Ⓥ

We found out. I hadn't expected Avarillo to come with me really, when I said it, but he came anyway. We corralled Wylie's horse where it had run a couple of miles from the scene of the ruckus, and tied his body across the saddle. The trail took us through the

117

Santiago, and we reached there about sundown, finding the house deserted, and no fresh sign. We went out through the cave that night, and up to Butcherknife, where we spent the night in the empty line shack there. T.S.A. evidently hadn't gotten around to putting another man on those cattle. We reached Alpine by early afternoon of the third day.

We rode down the middle of Main, leading Wylie slung across his horse, head down. I went near enough the curb, passing Cecile's Café, to see in through the dusty panes of the front window. It wasn't very busy this time of day. There was only one other customer besides Spanish Jack. Jack was holding Cecile's hand and leaning across the counter, and I could see those chalky teeth of his shining in that smile from where I was.

He didn't see us pass, but there was a crowd gathering around our horses as soon as I stopped them in front of Si Samson's stable. The coroner came over in a few minutes, a fat, pompous little busybody with a carnation in the buttonhole of his funeral-colored fustian. He took charge of the body, and I went over and sent a couple of wires at the telegraph office.

From the telegraph office, I saw Spanish Jack come out of the café and cut across Main toward the coroner's. Avarillo wanted to clean up first, but I dragged him, tired and dusty and pouting like a child, to the café. Cecile was behind the counter, when we came in, and gave me that smile, but somehow it wasn't the same after the Scorpion.

"You look tired, Marshal," she said.

"Big job of work about done," I said, sitting down and shoving back my hat to rub my eyes.

"About done?"

118

"Judge Kerreway never did come in for that second inquest, did he?" I asked.

She shook her head, watching me.

I hooked a menu and studied it. "He'll come in now. I just sent him a wire. This thing's ready to bust apart at the seams, and a lot of interesting yaks are going to pop out, when it does, including most of them connected with T.S.A.."

"T.S.A.?"

"Yeah. Give me some of that beef stew, will you? What're you having, Ignacio?"

"If you have it," he told Cecile, but looking at me, "I'll take a big, stiff jolt of tequila."

She wasn't as talkative as she was that first time. After she brought stew for both of us, she went back to the kitchen, and Avarillo poked me in the ribs with his elbow.

"If it is true that a closed mouth catches no flies, Marshal," he said, "you must be choking to death on them by now."

"I just thought it was about time we stirred up a little activity," I told him. "I'm getting tired chasing around all over Texas after the jaspers mixed up in this murder. It's about time a few of them came to me."

They did. They came in the late afternoon. Avarillo and I had a double at the front end of the Alpine Lodge's second story, and, waiting by the window, I saw the three horses pull up to the hitch rack below. Spanish Jack forked a shiny black with four white socks that looked like it had more flash than bottom. He swung out of his silver-mounted saddle with a flourish. Jerry Hammer climbed off his Copperbottom Quarter animal with as little effort as possible. I had never seen the third man before.

119

"I think Kelly Striker's come to pay us a visit," I said. "You got that stingy gun of yours?"

"But, of course," he said, chuckling. "One does not travel without one's friends."

There was a knock on the door after a time. I opened it and let them in. The one I had never seen before was standing in front of Hammer and Spanish Jack. He was a big man, pompous as a grain-fed steer, shoving his gut out and planting his custom Hyers wide apart, so you couldn't miss how important he was. The flesh of his face looked like inch-thick beefsteak rare, and his bloodshot eyes had gazed down the neck of a lot of good bottles. And yet, somehow, they held a little glow in them, and I got the idea the results of rich living only hid what was beneath.

"Kelly Striker," he said officiously, introducing himself. The two words sounded like somebody shoving a pair of Forty-Four flat noses home in the cylinder of a Colt. "I would have made your acquaintance sooner, Marshal, but you left in such a hurry last time."

"Business," I said. "Maybe you'd like to hear about your man?"

"Spanish Jack's man," Striker corrected me, stepping in as I moved back.

"Oh," I said. "You've just come along for the ride?"

"I hold a natural interest in what goes on in Alpine," he said. "What *did* happen to Bryce Wylie?"

"I came across him blotting some brands off T.S.A. beef down by Butcherknife," I told Striker. "He wanted to make it a corpse-and-cartridge occasion. He did."

A little muscle twitched beneath that beefsteak flesh of his cheek, and he couldn't control the momentary, instinctive shift of his eyes around to Jack. The sheriff couldn't hide his surprise, either. Striker's glance rode

120

back to me. He pulled back his coat to shove his thumbs behind the cartridge belt crossing his pin-striped pants, and thrust his gut out farther, walking to the window and staring down into the street.

"I can't feature that, somehow," he said. "Wylie was making a hundred and fifty a month as a deputy. Why should he risk his job for a few rustled beefs?"

I didn't answer. Avarillo was sitting on the bed, staring at me in a puzzled way. Jerry Hammer leaned against the door frame, building himself a smoke. I felt like a hide pinned to the wall with those empty, unblinking, little eyes on me.

"Are you sure?" said Kelly Striker, putting so much pressure on his gun belt with those thumbs that it creaked. He turned back to me. "Are you sure this didn't just happen on the road, somewhere? Wylie wasn't the kind to forget what you did to him at Cecile's."

"Wasn't he?" I said.

Striker took a heavy, labored breath, like a horse that had lost its wind. "A public officer shot a man down in Duval County about six years ago over a personal affair like that, and it caused him quite a lot of trouble. A mob wanted to hang him. He was put on trial. He was acquitted, but they removed him from office, and he had to leave Texas."

"Folks don't mind a man doing his duty," said Jack, shifting his weight from one leg to the other, like a fiddling stud. "But when he uses his office to settle personal differences. . . ."

He was a high-strung man to begin with, of course. I wondered if he was this nervous all the time, though. I found the tail of my eye on those womanish hands of his, waiting for that fluttering movement.

"Yes," interrupted Striker, "Wylie was well liked

121

around here, Welles. If it got to drifting around that things had happened that way, I'm afraid it wouldn't go so well with you."

"You seem to be working up some kind of beef," I said.

"I'm only interested in the welfare of this community," he said. "Mob violence is a terrible thing. Even if it wasn't a personal grudge between you two, Washington might question the affair rather closely, if the wrong kind of rumors reached them. Now I have no doubt it happened just the way you said. But for your own protection, Marshal, I think it would be wise to retire. I have connections in Washington. It could be done with no taint on your record. We could just move you onto another job, and get a fresh marshal out here."

"No," I said, "I can't see it that way. I'm too close to cracking this thing. I've got too much evidence another marshal couldn't use the way I can. It's going to bust higher than a broomtail hauling hell out of its shuck, Striker. It's going to shake a lot of men loose from their kaks."

Striker took another hoarse breath. "Won't you reconsider?"

Hammer had a last puff on his coffin nail, dropped it to the floor, ground it beneath a heel. Then he straightened from where he had leaned against the frame. The bedsprings creaked as Avarillo bent forward slightly. Jack's hands were motionless, at his sides.

"No," I said, and became conscious of the hard, cold feel of my own dewey against my belly. "I'll finish the ride."

"Oh?" said Striker. That little glow flared in his eyes.

I couldn't help keeping tabs on Jack's hands. I took in a breath and held it.

122

"Oh," said Striker again, and turned and walked out the door, and Jack and Hammer wheeled, and followed him.

## VIII

LIGHTS BEGAN TO POKE YELLOW HOLES IN THE evening along Main Street. Si Samson's livery doors groaned as he swung one shut against the rising chill. I stood at the window, hearing the creak of saddle leather as Striker and his boys mounted in front of the hitch rack below. Striker swung off north toward his home in the hills out there. Jack and Hammer trotted their animals around onto Second and out of sight. The jail was over there.

"I thought for a moment they were going to make a play," said Avarillo, still sitting on the bed. His eyes dropped to the walnut handle of my Cloverleaf. "They say Jack is a dangerous man. Even Hagar has a healthy respect for him."

"I've got his number," I said.

Avarillo chuckled. "I was beginning to lose my faith in you, when you talked like that in Cecile's. I think now, however, I perceive a pattern. You thought she would pass it on?"

"Didn't you see Jack sparking her when we passed?" I asked.

"And you think Striker found out what was in that wire you sent?"

"I hope he did," I said. "T.S.A. has their headquarters in Waco. That's where I sent the wire. I asked the marshal's office to dispatch a government auditor to check over T.S.A.'s books. The Scorpion gave me that idea. If Striker did have the influence to find out what

123

was in the wire, and T.S.A.'s books are shaky, I figured it would put a bee in Striker's bonnet."

"His sombrero was buzzing pretty loudly when he came here," said Avarillo. "But why didn't you tell him where you really found Wylie?"

"He would know where I stand," I replied. "This way, he might figure I'm lying about Wylie, and that I really found Wylie with those mustangs and suspect Wylie's connection. But he isn't sure. He's confused. Have you ever seen a steer when it's confused? It gets boogered and stops figuring its moves. Then you can haze it just about anywhere you want. I figure we've hazed Striker right into our Blocker loop."

We had. We went downstairs and sat in the lobby of the Lodge where I could look out on Second Street. There was a Mexican *cantina* next door to the jail. In about fifteen minutes, Jerry Hammer came out and unhitched his own Copperbottom and Jack's stockinged black, leading them across to Si Samson's stable. He came out of the stable and went back to the jail. The lights in the front room of the jail went off in a minute. We went out and crossed Main, going between two houses on the opposite side of the street to an alley behind. There, under a cottonwood, we waited. In another ten minutes, Hammer came up the alley farther down and went in the back door of the livery barn. He came out, riding his own horse and leading Jack's.

"A childishly elaborate plan to deceive us," said Avarillo at my side, and chuckled. That chuckle shook his kettle-gut. "When do we get our horses, Marshal?"

"Right now," I said.

Si Samson came out of the little room he had up front, when we hit the barn, scratching his roached mane and grumbling. "More damn horses coming and

124

going than I ever seed in Alpine before."

"Just got word Chisos Owens is gut-shot and dying down in the Santiago," I told him.

He looked at me with a strange, tight expression, then snorted, and turned back up the aisle to get our horses. Avarillo sighed heavily.

"What new, diabolical plan has the mad marshal in mind?"

"What do you figure the Scorpion would do, if she found out Chisos Owens was dying somewhere?"

"Go there," he muttered.

"That's what I figure," I said. "The way the grapevine works around here, she ought to hear about this before we get out of town."

Even his smile was fat. "It is surprising, how fast word can travel in such a desolate country. But then, most of the people are her friends. But why the Santiago?"

"When the Scorpion first came on me down there in the house, she asked for Kelly, before she saw me," I told him. "They had made it a meeting place."

Si brought back our horses. We filled our canteens at the water trough outside, then headed north out of town, past the cattle chutes at the railroad yards. I didn't bother trying to track Spanish Jack and his deputy, figuring they would meet somewhere near Striker's house. We topped the first rise and saw them in the light of a rising moon about a half mile ahead. Striker's home hunkered in a big grove of trees off the road at the crest of the next hill. A horse was coming down the road from there. It met Jack and Hammer at the wooden bridge crossing Calamity Creek in the cut. They all headed south, around town and on down toward Butcherknife.

125

The road followed Calamity Creek down to where it turned west just above Butcherknife Hills, the road bending east toward the Santiagos then, away from the creek. It was the only main route south, and we didn't bother keeping Striker and the others in sight, just trailing behind them most of the time, but checking up on their tracks once in a while and traveling the brush beside the road in case he sent one of his boys back to see if they were being followed.

We followed Chalk Draw down into where Crimson Cañon opened out, and then into that red cut, with its brush so thick that every foot was a battle. We could see by the moonlight and starshine indication where Striker and the others had forced their way through ahead of us—mesquite berries newly torn off their brush and recent horse droppings in the decay underfoot.

It was nearly dawn when we reached the end of the cañon. The brush thinned here, and the cañon opened up into sort of a bowl. The mouth of the mine was on one side of the bowl, so covered by tangled chaparral and devil's head that no one would suspect it was there if they didn't know about it.

One of the ears on Avarillo's mule flopped toward the cave. "¿Que pasa, querida?" he asked the critter.

"You cover me," I told him, getting off with as little noise as possible. "Striker might have left one of them behind."

I snuggled around the outside edge of the bowl, keeping in as much brush as possible, till I reached the mouth of the mine. There I could hear what the mule must have. It was a heavy, labored sound, like someone breathing. It stopped, after a minute. It took me a long time to get through without making any noise. With the last bit of brush still screening me from the inside of the mine, I could see him. Dim light from the sky filtered through to reveal his body stretched out, face down on the floor.

"I got my dewey on you, Hammer," I told him. "If you're dealing one from the bottom, you'll get your lights put out."

He made an effort to lift his head, failed, groaned heavily.

I crawled out with my lead chucker pointed at him. Crouching beside him, I turned him over. It looked like a whole herd of Texas longhorns had walked across his face. I had never seen such a bloody mess. His shirt was ripped down off his chest, and I got a good look at those muscles. They were like thick slabs of quilting covering his body, and one shoulder was bared like half a Webb County cantaloupe.

"It must have been about ten men," I said.

"Owens." It was hard to understand him through his smashed lips. "Chisos Owens. Striker left me to guard this end of the cave. Owens came through like you did. I tried to stop him. . . ."

"Like trying to stop a stampede," I said.

He didn't answer, and then I saw he had passed out. I went back and got Avarillo. We loaded Hammer on the rump of his mule, head down, and started picking our way through that shaft.

## IX

THERE IS NO MEASURING TIME IN A PLACE LIKE THAT. When we reached the other end, the first dawn light was beginning to silhouette the jagged outline of the Dead Horses across the valley. The windows of the house still in shadow made yellow rectangles against the darker

127

shape of the walls. We left our animals hitched to the corral a hundred yards behind the house, stretching Hammer out on the ground and tying his hands for good measure.

"Perhaps one of the shutters in back can be forced," suggested Avarillo.

Two wings of the house stretched out on either side of a flagstoned patio, with poplars growing around a dried-up well in the middle. We tried three windows along the south wing before a shutter gave. It was a bedroom, with a big four-poster at one side. I got my face full of cobwebs, climbing through. The door led to the hall. Cat-footing down this, we could begin to hear voices from the living room.

"Now wait a minute, Owens," said Kelly Striker, "you're taking too much for granted."

"On the contrary," said Owens. "Judge Kerreway wasn't going to sit on any second inquest, because there wasn't going to be any inquest. Powder Welles wondered why Jack issued that phony subpoena on me. I think I know why, Striker. You'd found out I was working at your Butcherknife line camp, and you were skeery I'd uncovered something, and you wanted to stop my mouth. Well, you were right, on all counts. Too bad T.S.A. is such a big organization. You can't keep your thumb on every department. Like Waco, for instance, where I signed on as Timothy Evans. They sent me to Butcherknife. And I *did* uncover something. A lot of things. There's another name on your Waco payroll sheet. Sam Skee. He used to work for a Kansas affiliate of T.S.A.. They were handling those rustled Mexican broncos."

"I can't believe it," said Striker. "If what you say is true, T.S.A. will take the necessary measures. . . ."

"Measures, hell," said Owens. "T.S.A. knew exactly

128

what was going on. Sam was busted up by one of them broncos, and drinks when it gets to hurting him, and talks when he drinks. He says there was a T.S.A. brand inspector on the Kansas company's corrals seven days a week. The inspector was working hand-in-glove with a colonel in the Quartermaster Corps who got a cut for not looking when they blotted the Mexican brands out with the Kansas company's mark."

Avarillo and I had now reached the end of the hall. The door here was partly open, and we could see the picture. Chisos Owens was standing before the front door, faced toward Striker and Spanish Jack, who stood by the table. The glass cover of that camphine lamp had been broken, when Elgera had swept it off the table that last time we were here, but it still worked. The light it shed, however, did not reach the other end of the room, and in the shadows over there, with the pale shine of her blonde hair and that strange glow in her blue eyes clearly visible, stood the Scorpion, whip and all.

"You seem to have all the data," said Kelly Striker.

"One word from me will start an investigation that will ruin T.S.A. and you along with it," said Owens.

"And that one word from you would pull Elgera Douglas right down with me," said Striker.

"That's as good as admitting it," said Owens.

Striker shrugged. "Why not? It will never get beyond this house. T.S.A. wiped out most of its resources in the battle to break the Scorpion down here. It would have folded up, if that order for mustangs hadn't come from the Army. But most of the other stock companies had gotten the jump on us and filled all the good sections with their own horse runners. We tried to wangle a deal with the Mexican government, but they wouldn't bite. The only thing left was to run the stuff across the

129

border. It was Jack here who got the idea of picking up the branded stuff. They were already broken, and that would save us the ten dollars a head it cost to have the wild ones busted."

Owens's face was pale and set. There was a little, ragged hole in the leg of his Levi's, high on the right thigh, and the faded cloth bore a dirty bloodstain there. That must have been where the gal's blue whistler caught him when he was skylighted in the door. Not too bad a wound, if he could stand on it like this so soon.

"What makes you think it won't get beyond this house?" he asked Striker.

Striker laughed confidently. "Elgera," he said.

Owens turned to the girl with a sick look on his face. "Tell me, Elgera, tell me just once. That's all I ask. I'll believe you. Anything you say."

"Tell you what?" asked Striker. "Are you still trying to convince yourself that she didn't murder Senator Bailes? Anything you say outside will just make it worse for her."

"He won't have to say *anything*, Kelly," I said, stepping in. "I heard it all."

Striker whirled toward me, surprised as a dogie the first time it's thrown, and all the angles must have passed through his mind in that moment. "Jack!" he shouted.

Jack had wheeled around, too, and had recovered from his surprise enough for his hands to make that fluttering movement. I hauled on my own dewey. The tips of his guns were just clearing the holsters when my first shot caught him. He grunted, and took a step forward, elbows twitching with the effort to lift the guns on up. I let another one go at the middle of him, and was twisting for Striker.

He was no gunny, and he had just fought his iron out. I

130

emptied my dewey into him. When his gun exploded, it was pointed the other way, because my shots had spun him around. He fell across Spanish Jack's body on the floor.

Then I saw someone coming at me from the other side of the room, and wheeled that way to see Chisos Owens. His lips were drawn back against his teeth, and his eyes held that gun-metal shine.

"That four-shot house gun don't quite go around, does it?" he said. "I'm sorry it's empty now. You aren't taking Elgera, Marshal. I told you that last time . . . no matter what she did . . . you're not taking her."

I guess he didn't know about my broken arm. Or maybe he would have done it anyway, feeling as he did about the girl.

"Chisos," I said, "don't. It won't be clean. I'm through fighting you clean. I'm taking that girl, and I don't care how I have to do it."

"No, you aren't," he said, going for his gun.

"Well, hell," I told him, and jumped in.

I had that empty Cloverleaf still in my good hand when I reached him, and I brought it down on his gun wrist with all my force. He howled in pain, and the Bisley went spinning out of his hand. He made a swipe at me with his other paw. It caught me on the side of the head as I jumped back. Ears ringing, I tore free and with that hand still held out toward me hit him across that wrist, too, with my dewey. He grunted hoarsely, pulling the hand back instinctively. It gave me an opening, and I wheeled in on that side, lashing him across the side of the face with the gun. It laid his cheek open. Blood spurting, he lurched toward me, trying to get a hold.

I dodged his arms again, and came in on the other flank. He whirled at me, but I caught him again, and jumped away. That one put a stripe across his forehead.

131

Shaking his head dazedly, he came on at me.

I took another shift that put me on the outside with him up against the wall. I slashed him on one side and then the other. I tried to get away, but each time he turned one way or the other. I kept driving him back with a blow, but finally he got too close and caught my broken arm. The pain blotted out sight for a minute. We were in against each other, and the smell of his blood almost gagged me. I slashed blindly at his head, felt him sag downward. He tried to catch my next blow with his free hand, but I changed directions and got past his block. He sagged again beneath the blow.

Yet, he wouldn't let go of that broken arm, and I guess I was crying like a baby with the agony of it now. I hit him again, and he slid farther down the wall. His face was up against my belly, but he still wouldn't let go of my arm. Bawling like a stampeded heifer, I still tried to tear loose, and lifted that Cloverleaf for another blow.

"If you hit him again, Marshal," said the Scorpion from behind me somewhere, "I swear, I'll kill you."

I stood there a minute, without turning around. Owens drew in a breath full of broken, hoarse pain. Then his grip on my arm relaxed, and he slid the rest of the way down the wall to sprawl at my feet. It came to me, then, that the Scorpion was still standing at the far end of the room by the fireplace, and there was no gun in her hand. I thought for a moment I'd been tricked. But the voice had come from *behind* me. Something made me turn that way.

The Scorpion, standing in the doorway, held that big Army Colt in her hand. But there was no whip dangling from her left wrist.

"Well," I said, "I should've figured this heifer for twins."

132

# X

BRANDING A COW WAS THE SMARTEST THING EVER done with the critters. I wished, somehow, that somebody had branded these two gals, so we could cut them out and chouse them to their right outfits. But then the brands would probably have been the same, anyway. Everything else was. They both had that hair, pale as a palomino's mane, and those blue eyes with the peculiar glow, and the suede *chivarras* with red roses down the seams. The curves on the one by the fireplace were more obvious and would probably have drawn a man's eye on the street quicker. But a little extra side-bacon doesn't always make a prize hog.

Avarillo had pulled his stingy gun when we first burst into the room, and that was apparently what had held the one over by the fireplace from any movement. But now he tucked it away with a strange, secretive chuckle, which gave the one in the doorway the drop on us.

"I shall relinquish my services now, Marshal," he grinned. "The problem which has presented itself is entirely yours."

"Pick Chisos up," said the one in the doorway, waving her gun.

I helped him onto a chair, where he sat with his head on his arms, making soft, retching sounds. I never knew a man to take such a beating and remain conscious. Spanish Jack was dead, but my two last shots had only caught Striker in the side, spinning him around that way. Avarillo helped me drag him over against the wall and sit him up, and the Mexican started to build a fire and heat some water for his wounds. Hagar was behind the woman with the Colt, and he moved around her, staring at the other one in a vague, puzzled way.

133

"Which one is the Scorpion, Hagar?" I asked.

He jerked his narrow head at the one with the Colt. "This one, of course."

"Are you sure?" said the one by the fireplace in that husky voice. "Are you sure, Johnny?"

He started to speak angrily, then checked himself. The one by the fireplace laughed throatily.

"The way I got it figured," I said, "Striker didn't take everyone on the board of directors of T.S.A. into his confidence when he started running these Mexican mustangs across. Bailes was one of those on the board who wouldn't have accepted it. But he was also in a position to uncover it, if anything aroused his suspicions. And that's just what he had done when he sent that wire from Alpine to Washington, assuring them that he had evidence which would stop the mustang running. Striker had to stop him or be ruined. Striker had been trying to break the Scorpion down here a long time, and this gave him a chance to kill two birds. He imported a gal from somewhere who was the Scorpion's double. He had her ride into town and kill Bailes, which naturally put the genuine Scorpion out among the willows."

"That's very clever," said Avarillo, "but, if Hagar, who has known her for years and who has been in love with her, cannot tell, in the final analysis, which one is the real Scorpion, how are you going to decide?"

"Let's all go outside . . . except for Chisos," I said.

The one with the Colt finally agreed. Owens's dun with the arched mane and Hagar's apron-faced horse were out there, along with Spanish Jack's black and Striker's animal. And two palomino mares. One was hitched to a support of the porch roof. I unhitched her and led her away from the house in case of a ruckus.

134

Then I put my foot in the ox-yoke and swung aboard. She was a spirited beast, and started side-stepping and cavorting, but I didn't have too much trouble handling her. I dismounted and ground-hitched her. Then I went over toward the mare hooked to a cottonwood some yards from the house. This one started snorting and hauling at its bridle before I was within ten feet. The nostrils fluttered, and the eyes rolled at me like shiny glass. The muscles began to ripple and twitch beneath its fine, pale skin.

"All right," I told the girl who had stood by the fireplace. "You step in this tree."

Her lips pinched in for a minute. Then she shrugged and walked toward the horse. The animal jumped around the same as it had before, fuming and whinnying. It allowed the gal to unhook it, though, and throw the reins over its head. But when she lifted her foot to the stirrup, it spun away.

With a curse like a man, she hauled on the reins. The spade bit in the critter's mouth caused it to wheel back fast with that vicious jerk on the reins. The girl jumped on its back without using stirrups. She hadn't found them when the buttermilk horse started chinning the moon. It cat-backed and double-shuffled and then went into a high-binder that looked fit to split a cloud. Coming out of that, it sunfished with such a violent wrench the girl lost her seat and spilled out of the yannigan bag. The horse galloped off a few hundred feet, wheeling around down there in nervous circles, snorting and squealing.

"How about you?" I told the one with the Colt.

She looked at me, then started walking toward the horse. We watched without saying anything. The girl on the ground sat up, shaking her head dazedly. The other

135

one reached the horse and looked like she was talking to it. Then she stepped on and brought it back to us in the prettiest little Spanish walk I ever saw.

I moved over to the gal on the ground. "You're under arrest," I said, "for the murder of Senator Warren Bailes."

Ⓥ Ⓥ Ⓥ Ⓥ Ⓥ

Rae Stewart was her name. She told us the whole story. She had been a rodeo queen. I figured it would take some kind of tough one like that to go through with Striker's plan—she had been love with Striker in Waco, and he had enough influence over her to rope her in on this roundup. She and Striker had been using this house as a rendezvous after Elgera Douglas had been forced into the tulles by the law. Rae was the one who had shot Chisos Owens here at the Santiago that time. It was the real Scorpion who had picked me up out on the Comanche Trail and had taken me to Avarillo's, and who had saved me from getting my lights put out by Bryce Wylie. She had been trailing the herd of mustangs Wylie was driving that time. Instead of driving them herself, she had been waiting till they got up around Alpine, so she could stampede them again the way she had that other herd, in the hopes of breaking up the rustling and exposing Striker's connection.

We all had some much-needed shut-eye at the Santiago, and a good breakfast the next morning. Striker's wounds weren't so bad that he couldn't stand the ride north. I took the horses down to the creek for water just before we left, and Elgera said she'd show me the good places.

"That was clever about *La Rubia*," she said.

"That means The Blonde, doesn't it?" I said. "I'd

136

heard you were the only one who could fork that buttermilk horse of yours."

"Si Samson sent one of his stable boys down to the Rosillos with news that Chisos was dying here," she said. "You did that on purpose?"

"That grapevine you've got should make Morse blush for shame," I told her. "I figured you'd fog in, if you heard the man you loved was sacking his saddle."

"He's just a very good friend," she said.

"Hagar, too, I suppose," I said.

She nodded, pouting a little.

"How about that time down in the Dead Horses with Wylie?" I asked.

"Don't thank me," she said.

"I'm not talking about how you saved my life," I said. "You know what I'm talking about."

"All right," she answered. "How about it?"

"Was it ever like that . . . with Chisos . . . or Hagar?" I asked.

She started to answer, then closed her mouth. The pout grew.

"I guess not," I said, and did what I'd been talking about again.

When I stopped kissing her, the lids of her eyes were dropped heavily, like a sleepy kid's, and she was staring at me with the same expression on her face I'd seen down in the Dead Horses that time.

"I've got a little duty to do," I told her. "But I'll be back."

"I'm not making any promises, Powder," she said.

"I am," I told her. "I'll be back."

"Snuffy little bronco," she said, "aren't you?"

137

# THE GHOST OF JEAN LAFITTE

*This short novel was the first story Les Savage, Jr., set in the Gulf Coast region of East Texas in the bayou country, the same setting to be found in his later novel, **Copper Bluffs** (Circle Ⓥ Westerns, 1996). This story was purchased by Fiction House on February 6, 1945 and appeared in the Fall, 1945 issue of **Action Stories** under the title "Tonight the Phantoms Ride." The author's title and text were first restored for its appearance in **The Morrow Anthology of Great Western Short Stories** (Morrow, 1997) edited by Jon Tuska and Vicki Piekarski, and it is that restored text which follows.*

## I

THEY WOULDN'T TAKE HIM ALIVE. ERNIE DENVERS had decided that even before the bay horse had gone down beneath him. Whatever else happened, they wouldn't take him alive. He stood there beside the dying animal, nauseated by the foul odor of rotten mud that rose from the bayou to his left, surrounded by the hollow booming of frogs from the pipestem canebrake at his back. So this was Texas. A helluva place. Why hadn't he chosen Wyoming, or Kansas? No. He had to pick Texas. East Texas at that.

His dust-grimed face became alert at the faint sound that rode the wind down his back trail. Them? He turned with a curse, breaking through the first canes. Who

138

else? They had been on his tail all last night and all today. They wouldn't give up now.

He might have stood five six, Ernie Denvers, fighting his way through the clattering brake, but there was something ineffably potent about his square, compact body that precluded any appearance of smallness. A three days' beard made a blue stubble-shadow over his adamant chin, and his eyes burned, red-rimmed and feverish beneath the straight black line of his heavy brow. He had no chaps, and the canes scraped his dust-grayed Levi's with an incessant, maddening clatter that knotted his nerves up inside him like snubbed dally ropes. Well, why not? A man that had been chased as long as he. Why not? They wouldn't get him alive, that's all. They wouldn't.

He whirled around to the sudden crash of pipestem canes at his side, and his reaction was automatic. The girl stood there, looking at him for a moment, and then a strange, wild smile caught at one corner of the fullest lips he had ever seen, and her eyes dropped to the big Artillery Colt in his hand. "You get it out pretty quick," she said.

Her hair was black and lustrous as the water in the bayous, hanging thick and tangled about the shoulders of a flannel shirt that was as old and tattered as the denim pants she wore. Her dirty Hyer boots were run over at the heels as if she did more walking than riding. She cocked her small head to the faint sound through the thicket behind them, and her black eyes flashed excitedly. "You're running from Giddings?"

"Giddings?" he said.

"Navarra was expecting you tonight," she said. "Uncle Caesar sent me out to meet you. He thought you might have trouble with Giddings, but he didn't expect

139

you to come this way."

"I didn't choose the way," he said warily.

"I understand." Her laugh bubbled up from inside, like there was a lot of it down there, and then she caught his arm. "I'll show you the way. We can reach the house before Giddings does. Navarra will take care of the rest."

He pulled back for a moment, but her hand on his arm was insistent, and she was already turning to brush aside the pipestems. What was the difference? He didn't know why this was, but it looked better than what he'd been seeing. Nor could he guess how long they ran through the canes. It was all the same. Rattling pipestems beating against his face and salt grass whipping across his legs and the booming frogs never still. She stopped abruptly, and he couldn't help being brought up against her and was surprised at the clean sweet smell of her hair. It seemed out of place, somehow, in all the other odors of putrescent mud and decaying vegetation that rose humidly from the bayou they had reached. She took his hand again and led him across the shaky bank through a grove of gnarled cypress trees, festooned with streamers of Spanish moss that slapped wetly across his shoulders. Then the first of the breeze struck him, carrying the faint tang of salt air, and in a few more moments he was surprised to find the mud turning to sand beneath his feet. Had he been that near the coast?

"Dagger Point," said the girl, gesturing toward the row of breakers gleaming dully from the darkness ahead. "It's neap tide now, and we can wade across to Matagorda Island. Take off your boots."

Shrugging, he slipped off dirty Justins, rolled up his Levi's on lean, hairy calves. Again he had no measure of time or distance. The water was never more than knee high, except for the rollers that foamed up over his waist. But he jumped these, and farther out they ceased, and he was wading through quiet water. When the breakers began again, they were going the other way, and finally Denvers and the girl were standing on the wet sand of that shore. She led him over dunes bearded with thick sea grass and then through the higher bunch grass of the coastal prairie, and finally he saw the house, surrounded by a brooding cypress grove. It was old Colonial, with the tall columns along its front porch peeling white paint that must have been put on thirty years before. Its shuttered windows stared blankly from warped weather boarding, and the porch floor popped dismally to their boots and the huge, oaken front door swung in on creaking hinges to a dim, musty reception hall.

Denvers wiped sweating hands across his Levi's. All right. She took him into what he thought was the parlor, high-ceilinged and heavily carpeted, filled with the same nameless sense of belonging to the past. There was a pair of Chippendale sofas facing each other in front of the fireplace, the harateen covering on their camel backs frayed and shiny, the *cabriolé* legs bearing scars that looked as if they might have come from spurs. The man stood beside a Pembroke table to one side of the hearth. The first thing Denvers saw was the thick streak of white through his jet black hair then his face, heavy-boned and heavily fleshed with an indefinable dissolution. The thick lids of his eyes were turned a shadowed blue by the network of tiny veins patterning them and only added to the leashed violence slumbering in the eyes themselves. His shoulders filled out the tailored cut of his long black coat well enough, and

141

Denvers couldn't see where he packed any gun. The spurs on his polished cavalry boots made a small tinkling sound as he shifted away from the table.

"He was way south of Dagger Point, Navarra," said the girl. "I heard him in the canes. Giddings was right behind him."

So this was Navarra, thought Denver, and watched the man come forward, wondering how such a heavy *hombre* could move with such apparent ease. Navarra bent slightly to peer at Denvers, and for a moment Denvers saw the anger rise in his eyes, enlarging the black pupils, and then the heavy bluish lids narrowed like a veil and whatever the man felt was hidden.

"This isn't Prieto," Navarra told the girl, and his voice held the same slumberous violence as his eyes. "What's the idea, Esther?"

The girl's small hand rose in a confused gesture. "You said he'd be there and might have trouble with Giddings. What else . . . ?"

Navarra turned to Denvers impatiently. "You have a name, I suppose?"

"Denvers," said Ernie.

"You want me to keel him, Sinton?" Denvers hadn't heard the Mexican enter the room. He was barefooted, standing over by a serpentine chest of drawers. He had a pair of longhorn *mustachios* that flapped against a dirty white shirt, and his eyes glittered like a sidewinder's from beneath a huge straw sombrero. "I got my gets-the-guts all sharpened up." He grinned evilly, running his brown finger down the blade of a *saca de tripas* he held. "Nobody hears me keel 'im. Nobody knows."

"Shut up, Carnicero," said Sinton Navarra, and then his head rose to the sound of snorting horses outside, and Denvers's move toward the door was automatic

142

because he knew who had come.

"No, *señor*," said Carnicero, moving in front of him with the knife. "I think you better stay, eh?"

"Out of my way," said Denvers.

"He can pull a gun pretty fast," said the girl.

"I can stick him before he gets it out," grinned Carnicero.

"Go and let them in, Esther," Navarra told the girl.

Denvers heard her move behind him and took a jump to one side, hauling at his big Artillery Colt. The Mexican threw himself at Denvers, heavy body hitting him before Denvers had his gun out.

"Carnicero!" shouted Navarra.

Denvers had to let go his gun, jerking up both hands to grab the Mexican's knife arm as it came down. With one hand on Carnicero's wrist and the other at his elbow, Denvers straightened the arm, using it as a lever to heave the Mexican backward against the wall.

"I have a gun pointed at your back, Mister Denvers." Navarra's heavy voice stopped Ernie Denvers. "If you will, forget whatever ideas you have about your own gun, and back carefully toward the chair on the right-hand side of the fireplace, and sit down?"

The girl slipped out to the reception hall, and Denvers could hear the front door creak open as he backed stiffly toward the wing chair, squatting dirty and tattered in the shadows beyond the pair of couches. He knew the surprise must have shown on his face when he saw the gun Navarra held.

"A singular weapon, is it not?" smiled Navarra sardonically. "French, Mister Denvers. A Le Page pin-fire, seven millimeters, twenty shots. A man is a veritable arsenal with one of these. Don't you think it's ingenious? The cylinder, as you see, has two rows of

143

chambers, one set within the other, each row containing ten chambers. The inner set fires through the lower barrel, the outer set through the upper, and. . . ."

He stopped talking with a sudden, enigmatic smile and slipped the gun beneath his coat up by the shoulder. Denvers stiffened in the chair, not knowing whether he meant to rise or what, and then let his weight back down because he saw the futility of that. Sheriff Giddings must have stood six four, and he came into the room with an arrogant swagger that pushed his heavy belly against his crossed gun belts and that caused the batwings on his *chaparejos* to flap with a soft, leathery sound every time he took a step. The red strings of a Bull Durham sack dangled across the dirty star pinned on his buckskin ducking jacket.

"Good evening, Sheriff," said Navarra easily.

"Not so good, Navarra," said Giddings, stopping in the middle of the rug and hooking hammy thumbs into his gun belts to stand there swaybacked and self-conscious as he swept the room with eyes that were meant to be hard. They settled on Denvers, and then met Denvers's glance. It was the sheriff's patent intent to force Denvers to drop his gaze, but Denvers stared wide-eyed and waiting at Giddings's pale blue eyes, and finally Giddings's own gaze shifted uncertainly, and clearing his throat with a hoarse, blustering sound, he looked jerkily toward Navarra. "No. As I say, not a very good evening. Jale Hardwycke was murdered last night."

"Oh." Sinton Navarra's velvety tone rose at the end of the word, and he pursed sensuous lips. "Too bad. What brings you here?"

"We caught the killers red-handed last night on the old Karankawa Trail out of Refugio. Couple of

144

saddlebums. Starting them back toward town when they put up a ruckus. We killed one. The other got away. Trailed him as far as Indian Bog. I'm not going back without him, Navarra."

"Very commendable," said Navarra. "I still don't see how we figure in it."

The sheriff's two deputies shifted uneasily in the doorway. One of them was short and squatty as a razorback hog, his cartridge belt shoved down by a beer-keg belly, his wool shirt covered with mud and horse droppings and other filth. Denvers's hands tightened slowly on the chair arms. He even knew that deputy's name. Ollie Minster. He was the one who had killed Bud Richie. Remembering that moment brought back Denvers's rage so strongly that it blotted out the whole room like a roaring black curtain sweeping across his vision, and he could hear his own breathing grow heavy and harsh in the sudden, strained silence.

"You got a new man, haven't you?" said Giddings, looking at Denvers.

"So Hardwycke was killed," said Navarra, and his slumberous eyes passed across Denvers, and then he was watching Giddings. "Wart hogs go rooting around the outside of a bush, Sheriff, after their feed, when they could go straight in and save a lot of time."

Giddings flushed. "I ain't beating around any bushes. I'll have that man in the wing chair, Navarra."

"I'm glad you came to the point, Sheriff," said the other. "What makes you think this man is your murderer? You say you found them last night? It was singularly dark, as I remember, without a moon. Could you positively identify him?"

"I'd know the jaspers anywhere," growled Giddings. "Two of 'em. Acted all right at first. Even gave us

145

names. Ernie Denvers and Bud Richie. Then, when we started figuring them in the murder, they got cagey."

"Names don't mean much," said Navarra. "Faces?"

Giddings jerked his head from side to side in a vague, evasive way, finally shrugging his arrogant shoulders. "Like you say, it was dark. Scuffling around and such, I didn't get much look at their faces. But this is him, I tell you. Denvers. Same height, same build."

Navarra's smile was sardonic. "Esther's about the same height as our friend in the chair."

"This *hombre* wasn't Texan," said Giddings. "He didn't talk Texas, and he didn't dress Texas. No leather leggin's, no ducking jacket. His hat was flat topped, and his pants was denim. . . ."

"Esther wears denims," said Navarra.

Giddings bent forward sharply. "You trying to say that Esther . . . ?"

"Don't be obtuse." The contempt gave Navarra's words a hissing intonation. "How could Esther have been there? I'm only trying to point out that you aren't really sure of anything concerning this man, Denvers. It could have been Esther, from all the descriptions you give, or a hundred other men in the vicinity. I don't talk Texas. Everybody in this state doesn't wear a center-creased Stetson and leather leggin's. You could find a dozen men tonight that look like this man in the dark. In fact, Jale Hardwycke and I are about the same height and build. Could you have told us apart last night? How do you know it was Hardwycke who was killed?

"Don't be a fool!" shouted Giddings apoplectically. "I know Jale Hardwycke when I see him. He'd been to Refugio and taken twelve hundred dollars cash out of the bank. We found his wallet with the money in it on this Bud Richie."

146

Denvers caught the sudden flicker of Navarra's eyes before his thick, bluish lids closed across whatever had been there. "Oh, the wallet. You have it now, then."

Giddings jerked his head from side to side that way then blustered: "No, dammit. I found Hardwycke's wallet on this Bud Richie and put it in my saddlebags as evidence. Then the ruckus started, and Richie got in the way of Ollie's bullet, and the Denvers jasper got away on my horse. Now, don't try to block me, Navarra. I'm taking this man."

"Did you see your horse outside?" said Navarra.

Giddings's voice was rising. "I said don't try to block me. I know you ain't fool enough to leave the animal showing. This is the only place he could have come."

"You're throwing your rope on the wrong steer, Giddings," said Navarra, moving in front of Denvers. "This man's been here since Tuesday."

"Has he?" said Giddings. "We'll find out soon enough. He'll have Hardwycke's wallet. I'm searching him."

"He's my guest, Sheriff," said Navarra, and his voice was velvety. "I wouldn't allow you to search him any more than I'd allow you to search me."

Blood flooded up Giddings's thick neck. "You and Caesar Sheridan think you're safe from the law, hiding out here on Matagorda Island, but you're under my jurisdiction just as much as any man in Refugio."

"Am I?" said Navarra sardonically. "I'm surprised you even came this far, Sheriff. The last lawman to reach Indian Bog was found dead. I'd be more careful, if I were you."

"I'll get you for that one, too, Navarra."

"Do you think I perpetrate every crime that happens within a hundred miles of Matagorda?" asked Navarra.

147

"These things were going on a long time before I came, Giddings, and will continue long after I'm gone. I think I'm the least worry you have when you're around Indian Bog, and I think you know that. Do you think you could get back across the channel with this man? Do you think you can get back alone?"

"Damn you, Navarra!" Giddings almost screamed it and took one lurching step toward Navarra with his hands held out. Then he stopped. A small vein had begun to pulse faintly across Navarra's temple, and Denvers could see his eyes. They were like the eyes of an enraged cat. The pupils were dilated until they showed black and feline between the heavy, blue-shadowed lids, flickering with an odd, ebullient light. Giddings stood there on his tiptoes, looking into those eyes, and his lower lip sagged slightly, and he began to pull his hands back toward himself in a strange, dazed way.

"I keel 'im, Sinton?" said Carnicero.

"I'm glad you didn't touch me, Giddings," said Navarra, running a pale, veined hand over that white streak through his hair. "Don't ever touch me. Don't ever lay your hands on me. It would be most unfortunate for you. Now, I'll ask you to go. You can't take this man from my house without a warrant. You can't even enter my house without a warrant, as a matter of fact."

Giddings's breathing had the driven, grating sound of a blown horse. He stood there for another instant, staring at Navarra. Finally he spoke, and his voice shook with his frustrated anger. "I'm coming back, Navarra. I'm coming back with enough warrants to send you and this whole household to hell! You've thrown your last dally on Matagorda!"

148

He whirled and stamped swaybacked out of the room, shaking the floor with each step, shoving his deputies ahead of him with a hoarse curse. His spurs clattered down the hall, the door slammed hard, and the squeak of saddle leather came faintly through the heavy red velvet curtaining the front windows. Denvers was on his feet by then.

"Why protect me like that?"

"Perhaps because of a singular dislike for our Sheriff Giddings," said Navarra, a soft ebullition in his smile. He held out his hand, a huge jade ring glinting on one finger. "And now, Denvers, the wallet. . . ."

The man coming through the door stopped him, voice filling the room like the roar of a rutting bull. "I saw Sheriff Giddings leaving, Navarra. Did he try to cause your man any trouble?"

"Prieto didn't come yet, Caesar," said Navarra.

The other glanced at Denvers. "Who's this, then?"

"I was waiting on the mainland for Prieto, like you told me, Uncle Caesar," said the girl. "I guess I brought the wrong one."

"Yes," said Navarra ironically. "Mister Denvers, would you meet Caesar Sheridan, Esther's uncle, the owner of this . . . ah . . . house, the ruler of Matagorda Island, the king of. . . ."

"Tie up your duffel, tie up your duffel," said Caesar Sheridan, waving one beefy hand disgustedly. He was a short man with enormously broad shoulders and a huge belly. His broad black belt pulled in tightly till a roll of fat slopped over it beneath his red wool shirt. He moved on into the room with short, quick steps, putting his boots down as if he wanted to poke their spiked heels through the floor. His face was puffy and discolored, purplish jowls patterned by a network of veins, eyes

149

bloodshot and bleary above their dark bags. His lusty, violent approach to life was in every movement, and his thick lips curled back off broken teeth when he spoke, jerking his close-cropped head toward Navarra. "What was Giddings here for then?"

Navarra's slumberous eyes slid to Denvers. "Giddings was hunting the murderer of Jale Hardwycke."

Caesar Sheridan looked at Denvers. "You kill Hardwycke?"

Denvers moved a hand helplessly. "I. . . ."

"Giddings must have been pretty sure to come this far," insinuated Navarra.

Sheridan threw back his scarred head and let out a laugh that made the crystal chandeliers tinkle above their heads. "Good for you, Denvers, good for you. I always hated that Hardwycke's guts. He thought all the land in Texas belonged to him just because he dealt in real estate. Always claiming we had no legal title to Matagorda. You must be pretty good with a gun, if you got him. Or did you do it drygulch style? Never mind, never mind. I don't care how you did it. Any man who finished Hardwycke's beans is good enough for me."

"It would be dangerous for him to go back to the mainland now," said Navarra softly.

"Dangerous?" roared Caesar Sheridan. "Hell, it would be suicide. Hardwycke was a big man on the coast. I'll bet they've got a dozen posses out combing the Gulf. How about signing on here, Denvers? I need a man with a gun like that."

Denvers looked toward Navarra. "You were saying something about the wallet?"

"Wallet?" said Navarra. "What wallet?"

150

## II

THE SAND OF DAGGER POINT SHIFTED RESTLESSLY under a mournful wind sweeping in off the Gulf of Mexico, and somewhere above the hoary crest of a grassed-over dune a sea fowl squawked plaintively at the night. Denvers had a time getting his paint mare into the first foamy breakers piling up on the shore, but finally she was splashing knee deep after Caesar Sheridan's fat bay. Carnicero shoved up beside Denvers on a shaggy old mule, forking a ratty Mexican-tree saddle.

"Why did Navarra start to ask me about the wallet last night?" said Denvers.

"How do I know?" said Carnicero. "You better not ask too many questions. You better be glad Sheridan let you stay on Matagorda."

"Who is Sheridan?" said Denvers. "He owns that house on the island? It was when he came in that Navarra seemed to forget about the wallet. He passed it off like it didn't matter. Did it?"

"You keep prying, and I keel you."

"That seems to be your only pastime," said Denvers. 'Carnicero means butcher, doesn't it?"

"Why else should they name me that?" said the Mexican. "It is my life. I was born with a *saca de tripas* in my hand. They pinned my swaddling clothes together with stilettos. I ate my *frijoles* with a Bowie knife from the time I was strong enough to lift it. When they gave me my first machete, I was so happy I went right out and killed my grandmother. You should see what I can do with a blade, *señor*. I could cut your ear off so deftly you wouldn't know it was gone till your hat began to slip down on that side of your head. Colonel James

151

Bowie himself could not slice a man into as many strips with one knife as I. . . ."

"Will you stop that gab," said Caesar Sheridan angrily. He halted his bay in the shallows breaking on the mainland shore, turning to Denvers. "Neap tide's in the channel now. About this time of year it lasts from midnight till dawn, and a man can wade across on foot at the shallow spots like Dagger Point. You saw how it was. Water didn't get above your stirrups. If you get separated from us on the mainland, just be sure you get back here before daylight. Miss neap tide and you're stuck on the mainland most of the day. Nobody can swim that channel when the water's in. There's a riptide that'll pull the strongest swimmer under. I've never seen a horse that could make it." He paused, looking ahead. "I guess this is Prieto."

The dim shadow emerged from the gloom shrouding the desolate beach, resolving itself into a horsebacker. As he drew closer, the faded denim ducking jacket became visible, hanging slack from the stooped shoulders of a tall man, and the *conchas* winked dully from the batwings of old bullhide chaps. Prieto had come in the night before, angry at not having been met on the mainland, and his voice was still acrimonious as he spoke. "Bunch of coasters grazing about two miles inland. Your man, Judah, made sure Sheriff Giddings was in Refugio."

Prieto fell in beside Sheridan, giving Denvers a close glance. Denvers caught a glimpse of the gaunt, acrid face with its bitter eyes and tight mouth. Denvers had gotten the impression last night that Prieto was new to Matagorda, and that he belonged to Navarra more than to Sheridan. Denvers wondered why Prieto should be over here tonight. Navarra wasn't.

152

They lined out of the water to cross the pale sand, and soon the salt grass was swishing at Denvers's *tapaderos*. Post oaks began to loom up out of the night, and they forded a bayou with the rotten mud sucking at the horses' fetlocks and the croaking of bullfrogs all around them. They were riding through a veritable swamp now, the rising moon casting a ghoulish light down through the moss-festooned trees. A bull 'gator bellowed somewhere out in the pipestem cane, and Denvers slapped continually at the mosquitoes that fogged the air around him. They finally reached a solid bit of ground where a giant mulatto was holding a train of Mexican rat mules.

"They still watering, Judah?" asked Prieto.

The mulatto nodded a bullet head set on a neck like a bull's, and the thick muscles across his bare chest caught the light wetly as he hitched at his white cotton pants. Sheridan slipped a Sharps carbine from his saddle boot, turning to Denvers.

"There's a bunch of coasters grazing and watering in that cypress grove farther on. We're downwind of them. We'll be able to get right close before they spot us. Drop as many as you can before they get out of the trees."

"*Drop* as many?" queried Denvers. "What kind of roundup is this?"

"It's the way we work," said Sheridan. "Any complaints?"

Denvers shrugged, loosing his big Artillery Colt in its worn holster. Sheridan booted his bay, leaning forward in the saddle, and worked through the cypresses. Following him with the others, Denvers finally made out the first coaster grazing in the tall salt grass, a big brindle steer with withers as sharp as a Barlow knife and

153

horns that gleamed like scimitars. The others were farther on, wallowing in the bayou that ran through the cypresses, feeding in the knee-high grass. Suddenly the brindle raised its head, turning toward the men.

"Let's go!" whooped Caesar Sheridan and flopped his *tapaderos* out wide to bring them back in against the bay with a solid, fleshy thump. The horse shot out of the trees, and Sheridan's rifle was already bellowing. The brindle let out a scream of mortal pain, whirling to stumble a few steps away from Sheridan, then sinking down into the muck. Denvers charged through the salt grass after Judah and Prieto, throwing down on the first beef he neared, a big, speckled heifer that got tangled up in the Spanish moss of a cypress when it tried to run. Denvers put two .44 slugs into it before the beast went down and then pulled up his paint and charged after another cow, guns thundering all around him, men bellowing as loudly as the cattle. Carnicero was on Denvers's flank, quartering into a big dun steer with a lobo stripe down its back. He got within ten feet of the animal, an ancient Navy pistol held above his head to throw down.

"Shoot dat steer," roared Judah, emptying a pair of six-shooters in wild volleys at the cattle, laughing uproariously every time a beef squalled and went down. "What's the matter with you, Butcher? Waiting foah him to come up and take the gun away from you? Shoot dat steer."

But Carnicero galloped on past the dun without firing, shouting something over his shoulder, and whirled to chase after a big black farther on. Denvers's paint stumbled in the muck, and the Spanish moss tore him backwards in the saddle. Struggling in the festoons of wet green growth, he whirled his paint out from among

154

the cypresses, breaking into the open with streamers of moss flung out behind him like dripping pennons. Suddenly Carnicero's mule stumbled and went down, and the Mexican went over his head, landing sprawled in the muck farther on. Judah came charging from the cypresses at one side, splashing into the bayou after a huge steer with blood streaming down its black hide. The giant mulatto had emptied his guns at it, but the beast was still going headlong. It tried to gain the trees again, bellowing frenziedly, but Judah quartered it, once more forcing the steer out into the shallow bayou. Squealing in rage and pain, it floundered straight toward Carnicero.

The Mexican got to his knees, mud dripping off his white pants, and brought up his old Navy. He drew a bead on the charging steer. Denvers thought all sound had stopped as he waited for the explosion of the Navy. Then he saw the strange fear cross Carnicero's face.

"I can't," he shouted in a cracked voice. "I can't shoot. Judah, get that crazy *cimarrón* before he runs me down."

"What's the matter?" roared Judah. "I can't get him. My guns are empty. Shoot him, you damn fool!"

The beast had gained momentum now and was bearing down on Carnicero, mud and water showering up back of its churning legs. Denvers spurred his paint into a floundering run through the bayou, slipping off solid land into the rotten muck with a loud popping sound, viscid mud shooting up into his face. He threw down on the steer, and the Colt jumped in his hand with a hollow click. Empty!

Carnicero was stumbling backward, knee deep in the muddy water, shouting in terror. Denvers dropped his empty Artillery into its holster and tore the lashing off

155

his dally, turning his horse so he would run in between Carnicero and the steer. But there were only a few feet left, and Denvers was about as far away from the two of them as the steer was from Carnicero. He knew he would never be able to cut in front of the steer before it reached the Mexican. He was close enough to see the terror in Carnicero's face. The steer loomed above the man, huge and black. Denvers had his loop swinging, and he leaned forward as he tossed. While the rope was still in the air, he jerked viciously to one side on the reins, thrusting his weight that way as the paint whirled, and, when the loop settled about those great horns, the horse was going full speed in the opposite direction from the steer. Denvers snubbed his rawhide dally on the slick horn, and the violent impact almost pulled his chunky paint off her feet, cinches cracking loudly with the strain, saddle jumping beneath Denvers.

He heard the steer let out a tremendous, raucous bawl, and then he was off the paint, leaving it to stand there with forefeet braced to keep the rope taut on the steer. At least they bred ropers in this god-forsaken swampland. The beef was on its back in the bayou, feet flailing, great horns sending up spouts of foul mud as it tossed its head wildly from side to side. Denvers stumbled toward the huge beef through the muck, jacking empties from his Artillery and thumbing in fresh ones. He waited till the tossing head was turned his way, and, as the steer lurched to get on its feet, he put a bullet between its bloodshot eyes. The beast suddenly stopped thrashing, and the rope went slack, and the tremendous black body sank back into the mud. Only then did Denvers see how close Carnicero was standing to the carcass. The Mexican hadn't moved from where he had been when the rope snubbed the steer, and he could

156

have reached out and touched the animal's wicked, curving horn. Carnicero opened his mouth, letting out a shaky laugh, lips working around his words for a moment before he could make any sound. Finally he swallowed, stuttering.

"*Barba del diablo*, if that *ladino* had come one more foot, I would have been hanging on those horns instead of your rope. Where did you learn to swing a dally like that, Denvers?" The blood had come back into his dark face by now, and the grin faded, and he began to pout like a sullen child. "*Pues*, just because you save my life, don't think I won't keel you the first chance I get."

Denvers laughed. "Why didn't you shoot that steer when you had the chance? It was pointblank. You couldn't have missed."

Carnicero's eyes lowered uncomfortably, and he wiped his nose, sniffling. "*Dios. Sacramento.* I got my powder wet in the mud, that's all. What else? I got my powder wet. *Sí.*"

Denvers took the Navy from his lax hand, spun the cylinder, then looked up at Carnicero, frowning. "What do you mean you got your powder wet? It didn't even touch the bog. This whole gun's as dry as the top of my hat."

### III

THEY HAD HAULED THE CARCASSES UP ONTO DRY land, and Judah dismounted after the last beef had been dragged in. Taking a long skinning knife from his belt, he started to slice a beef's hide down to its leg.

"You going to jerk the meat right here?" said Denvers.

"Jerk the meat?" laughed Judah. "Jerk the meat, he

157

says. Denvers, that meat ain't worth curing even. It's the hides. I guess you ain't been working this part of the country, eh? Two and a half cents a pound for beef in Kansas City. For what it costs to drive cows up there, you could make more profit on dirt. Cows ain't worth raising for their beef any more. Hides and tallow is all we take now. Where you come from, anyhow?"

"New Mexico," said Denvers.

"No wonder you don't know," said Judah. "You're right in the middle of the Skinning War, boy. Ain't you heard? A man in Refugio says that last year Texas shipped out three million dollars' worth of hides. How many hides is that, Butcher?"

"More than you'll ever be able to count," muttered Carnicero. "That ain't all. My cousin, he can read, and he saw in the *Galveston News* that a hundred million pounds of tallow was shipped out in Eighteen Seventy-Four. They don't have branding season any more in Texas. It's skinning season. Hides-and-tallow 'punchers we are now. Not cowpunchers."

"Quit blowing your air and get to work with that skinning blade, Butcher," said Caesar Sheridan.

"I tell you what," said Carnicero. "I'll haul them in, and you skin them."

"We've hauled them all in," growled Sheridan.

"There might be some we missed out there in the bayou."

"You get to work, dammit!" roared Sheridan.

"I hate to stain the blade of my knife with a cow's blood," pouted Carnicero.

"Maybe you never stained your blade with *any* blood," laughed Prieto.

"And maybe I keel you."

"Start skinning those hides," shouted Sheridan, rising

158

up from a carcass with his beefy hands dripping blood and tripe. "Or do you want me to take your hide across the bay with the cows?"

Mumbling incoherently, Carnicero moved toward the black steer Denvers had thrown. He took out his gets-the-guts, regarding the long slim blade with a mournful expression, then looked down at the steer. Denvers saw that his dark cheeks were wet.

"What's the matter with you?" yelled Sheridan.

"I can't," choked Carnicero and then began to cry like a baby. "*Madre de Dios*, I can't bear to think of cutting up this *pobrecito*. Such a pretty *bulto* he was, all black and young and strong. How would you like it if someone came along and shot you and took off your pretty *negro* hide? He never did anything to you. He never did anything to me. And now you want me to desecrate such a beautiful, wild creature by cutting him up."

Caesar Sheridan threw back his scarred, close-cropped head and sent the Spanish moss to fluttering with that thunderous laugh. Then he moved over to Carnicero in his quick, catty way, and shoved the Mexican toward the horse. "Go on, you old fool, haul them in if you like. I'll bet you never used that knife for anything more than eating *frijoles* with. 'Keel 'im'? You make me laugh. What happens when you come to using the knife on a man?"

"Oh, men are different," said Carnicero, his tears giving way to laughter with a sudden, child-like naïveté. "*Sí*, I slit their throats like this"—he drew his *saca de tripas* across his neck, chuckling—"I cut out their entrails with my gets-the-guts like this. I. . . ." He stopped with his *saca de tripas* pressed against his belly, and he was staring past Sheridan at something in the trees. Denvers followed the Mexican's glance. All he

159

caught was a shadowy motion through the cypresses, but Carnicero's voice was shaking with terror. "*Madre de Dios. ¡Espiritu de Lafitte!*"

Sheridan whirled to look. "Lafitte's ghost? Where?"

Cringing, the Mexican raised a shaking hand to point toward the trees. "You saw him. Right there, Caesar. Cocked hat and satin knee pants and gold buttons and all. You saw him. Cross yourselves, *compadres*. You are cursed unless you do. You will die like Arno Sheridan."

Caesar Sheridan grabbed Carnicero by the arm, jerking him toward the trees. "No ghost killed my brother. You're showing me this thing, once and for all. I'm tired of hearing these stories. Whatever put that sword through my brother was human, and I'm proving it. Did you see, Judah?"

The mulatto was bent forward, whites of his eyes gleaming from his black face, lower lip slack and wet. "Lawd, Caesar, I saw somethin'. Don't go in there."

Still hauling Carnicero toward the trees, Caesar bent to scoop up his Sharps with a free hand. "There isn't any ghost, I tell you. If you saw something, it's human, and I'm getting it this time or my name isn't Caesar Sheridan. Come on, you puking dogie, show me."

"No. *Dios*, no!" Carnicero tried to pull back. "You can't catch a ghost, Caesar. I saw it. Cocked hat and satin knee pants and . . . !"

Caesar hauled him over the hummock of ground between the two cypresses, and they dropped into the lowland beyond, disappearing in the grove. Denvers started to follow, but Prieto caught his arm. "Never mind. It won't do any good."

"Yeah," muttered Judah thickly. "How can you catch a ghost?"

160

"What are you talking about?" said Denvers. "This ghost."

"Lafitte's ghost," said Judah, looking over his shoulder. "You know, Jean Lafitte, the pirate? Who do you think built that house on Matagorda Island? It's where his mulatto mistress killed him. As long as there's a woman in that house, Lafitte's spirit is doomed to roam this coast. I've seen him before, over on the island. He'll kill us all, sooner or later, Denvers. You're crazy to stay on Matagorda. I'm crazy. I don't think I'll go back."

He whirled toward the cypresses, but it was only Carnicero, white pants dripping mud up to the knees as he came back through the trees. "Caesar caught sight of it again, and he was after it like a bull with a fly in his nose. I thought I'd come back."

"That was good work," said Prieto.

"But I really see the *espiritu*," said Carnicero huskily. "Right there between the trees. Lafitte's . . . !"

"I know, I know." Prieto waved a sinewy hand. "It was a good job. It got Sheridan away neat as a white Stetson."

"But I really saw the ghost!"

"Shut up," said Prieto. "We aren't talking about Lafitte's ghost. Sheridan's gone now, and we aren't talking about Lafitte's ghost."

A sudden grin flashed Judah's white teeth across his black face, and the thick muscles over his bare chest rippled as he flexed his arms, stepping toward Denvers. "That's right, Prieto. We better get it done before Caesar gets back."

Denvers noticed for the first time how the top of Prieto's holster was patterned with a myriad of faint scars that might have come from the man's fingernails

161

raking the leather over and over again, and he suddenly understood that Prieto hadn't come with them tonight for the cows. For this? For what? With that same childish shift of emotion, the fear had left Carnicero now, and he was grinning at Denvers, caressing his *saca de tripas*. All of them, then. Denvers felt his throat close on his breath, and sweat broke out on his forehead. "Get what done?"

"Hardwycke's wallet," said Prieto. His holster made a soft, leathery sound against his bullhide chaps as he took a step toward Denvers, and the thin line of his mouth was as acrid and bitter as his voice. "We want it, Denvers."

"Seems a lot of folks want that wallet," said Denvers, trying to watch them all at once. "What's in it, Prieto? Twelve hundred dollars couldn't be so interesting. Something more?"

The salt grass swished eerily beneath Judah's advancing bare feet. "You don't need to worry what's in it, Denvers. You givin' it to us, or we takin' it?"

Denvers understood fully now how it was, and he felt the spasmodic twitch of his hand curling above his gun. Three of them? He didn't think so. One, maybe, or even two, but not three. Not coming in from every side this way. Even if a man could pull his gun fast enough.

"I guess we're taking it," said Prieto.

The grass was wet beneath Denvers's feet, and a sudden shift of wind swept a streamer of Spanish moss between him and Prieto, and then swept it out again. Their faces were turned ghastly by the moon, leering at him as each of them continued to move in, the lines of their bodies growing tense.

"Good," chuckled Judah. "Better this way anyhow."

From the corner of his eyes Denvers caught the ripple

162

of Judah's heavy black chest. *All right, damn you.* Carnicero was easing his knife down, and Denvers had seen that kind of thrust before, used by all *saca de tripas'* men to rip a man's guts out. *All right.*

"I keel 'im?"

"You'll kill nobody," shouted Caesar Sheridan, plunging up out of the bayou on the other side, slapping the mud from his leggings with the barrel of his Sharps. "What's going on here?"

Prieto turned with a palpable spasm, forcing a weak smile. "Nothing, Caesar, nothing. Get him?"

"What do you think?" said Caesar disgustedly. He looked narrowly from Prieto to Denvers and then the others. "Why didn't you come?"

"Nobody could catch a ghost," said Carnicero sullenly.

"Ghost?" Caesar Sheridan looked out into the somber depths of the cypress grove, shot through with pale, eerie moonlight. Somewhere a cat screamed, like a woman in mortal pain. Caesar moved his enormous shoulders, as if shrugging off something. "Let's get back to the skinning."

Denvers stood there a long moment, watching Prieto walk stiffly toward his horse, seeing Judah turn toward a carcass with a tight frustration in the twist of his lips. Finally Denvers moved over to a dead steer, surprised to find himself trembling. Reaction? He shrugged. He didn't know. He did know it hadn't been finished here tonight. At least he'd be expecting it next time. He had started to bend over the beef, but he stopped. "Pothook," he said.

Caesar was stripping off a hide. "Eh?"

"I said this steer carries a Pothook brand," said Denvers. "Esther told me what few steers you run on the

163

island are marked with a Double S."

Caesar Sheridan's scarred, bullet head turned up. "So?"

"You got a bill of sale?"

Caesar straightened slowly, his long, thick arms hanging slightly forward from his squat, potbellied torso like a gorilla's. "And if I don't?"

"I might have known as much," said Denvers. "No wonder you made sure Sheriff Giddings was in Refugio tonight. I guess the bottom has really dropped out of the cattle business down here when a man rustles cows for their hides."

A slow grin spread Caesar's thick lips over his broken teeth. "You got your piggin' string on the right steer, Denvers. Now, get to work."

"I never took a cow that wasn't mine," said Denvers. "Even for the skin."

"You'd kill a man for a wallet that wasn't yours," said Caesar. "I think you'd better reconsider the cows."

"No," said Denvers. "I don't think I will."

Caesar Sheridan moved up to Denvers in that quick, catty way and stood there with his huge belly lopping over his tight belt. "You aren't in any position to be choosy, Denvers. The only reason you're safe, coming this far onto the mainland, is because we're with you and because we made sure Giddings and his posses weren't around this section of the coast. Try it alone and you'd run into those posses before your horse had time to dry the sea water off it. Or maybe you'd prefer a lynch rope."

"I'll take my chances," said Denvers, and turned toward the paint.

He was yanked back around by Sheridan's bloody hand on his collar and pulled violently up against

164

Sheridan's gross body, with the stink of blood and sweat and leather almost overpowering him. "Nobody's taking chances, Denvers, least of all me. If Giddings's posses caught you, you'd talk about tonight. I'm not having that. The only reason Giddings can't come on Matagorda with warrants for us is that he doesn't have anything to issue warrants for. The minute he gets positive proof of anything, that channel won't be any more protection to us than a mud fence after a big rain. And I'm not sending him that proof in the person of any witness tonight."

"Sheridan," said Denvers, "I'm leaving. Either you take your hand off me, or I'll take it off for you."

Denvers saw the slow flush creep into the man's sensual face, and for a moment the hand holding his collar trembled. Then Caesar Sheridan's lips drew back in that ugly grin. He threw back his close-cropped head and laughed. "You're not going anywhere," he roared. "And if you want to try it. . . ." His voice choked off in a gasp as Denvers's fist sank into his belly up to the wrist. Sheridan bent over spasmodically, and Denvers brought the same fist on up, smashing it into the hand holding his collar. With Sheridan's hand knocked away, Denvers swung his whole body into another blow at the man's gross belly. He felt his knuckles sink into the soft flesh until he thought they had gone through Sheridan. Caesar staggered backward, his face dead white, and twisted in a strange surprise, as if he hadn't believed a man Denvers's size could hit like that.

"I keel 'im," screamed Carnicero, and they were all in on him, shouting and yelling, Judah bringing his knee up against him and knocking him back into the salt grass. For a moment Denvers went to his knees beneath the weight of their bodies, fighting blindly, head rocking

165

to someone's boot smashing his mouth. Then Caesar Sheridan came in from somewhere, roaring like a bull, tearing Judah off with an open hand and sending him backward in a spin that crashed him into a cypress, rolling Prieto aside with a backward swipe across the face. "This is mine!" roared Sheridan, grabbing Denvers by the collar again and yanking him onto his feet. "This is mine!"

Denvers ducked the man's first blow without having seen it coming, felt Sheridan's arm go past his head, and slugged for that belly. He heard Sheridan gasp and tried to tear free of the man, but this time Sheridan had him. He threw his ponderous weight to one side, blocking Denvers's next fist, and Denvers was taken off balance. They both rolled into the salt grass, boots spewing viscid, black mud. Sheridan got on top of Denvers's back and jammed his face in the mud, riding him like a bronco, slugging the back of his neck. Face driven deeper into the muck with each blow, Denvers tried to take a gasping breath and choked on the mud. He writhed over on his back, mud blinding him, reaching up to catch Sheridan's fist as it came down.

Gripping the fist in both hands, he rolled again, carrying Sheridan off him, and then he was on top. Sheridan grabbed him in a bear hug, and for the first time Denvers felt the incredible, driving strength of the man. He was pulled against Sheridan's gross body, unable to hit him, ribs cracking and popping under the inexorable pressure of Sheridan's massive arms. Somehow Denvers got his forearm in between Sheridan and himself, forcing it up until his hand was across Sheridan's face with the heel against the man's nose. Gasping weakly, he shoved upward, forcing Sheridan's head back. Sheridan made a desperate, strangled sound,

166

rocking his scarred head from side to side in an effort to free himself, but Denvers kept his hand jammed against the man's nose, and finally, shouting in agony, Sheridan had to release his hug in order to tear himself away.

Denvers leaped up, the cypresses spinning around him, Prieto and Judah dim, unreal figures that seemed to sway toward him, bent forward with waiting leers on their warped faces. Then Sheridan was in front of him again, a massive wall moving in to crush him. Denvers spread his legs and once more sought the man's belly with his hard fists, trying to keep free of Sheridan's arms. He heard the man's gasps of pain every time he sank his knuckles into that roll of fat lopping over the broad black belt. Sheridan jumped back, sobbing for breath that wouldn't come, his crazy, roaring laugh echoing through the trees.

"By God, I haven't had a fight like this"—he broke off to grunt sickly, as Denvers struck again and jumped on backward, bent almost double, shaking his bullet head—"damn you, Denvers, I'll kill you!"

He took a blow in the face to come in close with Denvers and caught Denvers's next blow with both hands, grasping his arm and swinging him around to slam against a tree. Denvers tried to get his shoulder in between himself and Sheridan, but Sheridan caught Denvers's lank, black hair and began beating his head against the furrowed bole of the tree. Denvers heard someone's desperate shout, realized it was his own, and felt himself writhing helplessly against the weight of Sheridan's gross torso holding him against the cypress, still beating his head against the trunk that way, and then he couldn't hear anything any more but the roaring in his head, or see anything, or feel anything, and finally even the roaring was gone.

# IV

DENVERS'S FIRST CONSCIOUS SENSATION, PERHAPS, was that of being suffocated. He reached out his hand with a sob, trying to shove away the heavy crimson damask all around him. A cool hand caught his, forcing it gently down again. Then, beyond his muddy boots, he saw the white and gold footboards of the bed, stuffed with the same color damask, and above his head the pulleys which drew the drapery of the four-poster bed up, and finally the girl's face. She started to draw away, and he closed his hand on hers to keep her there. Then he felt the first real pain in his head, and it must have shown in his face, because her black eyes suddenly grew large with compassion.

"Nobody's ever whipped Uncle Caesar," she said. "You were a fool to try."

Denvers sat up, almost fell back, grabbed the fretted bedpost to keep himself erect. "Where's my gun?"

"I guess Uncle Caesar took it. He isn't mad at you, though. He's funny that way. He likes you all the better for standing up to him. He says you're the toughest"—she broke off to catch him as he tried to get up and almost fell on his face, stumbling against the marble-topped table by the window—"here, you can't do this . . . !"

"I'm getting out!"

She released him suddenly, allowing him to sink back onto the bed against the post, and her face was flushed. "The cattle?"

"I never ran wet cattle in my life, and I'm not starting now," he said. "Not even wet hides."

"I know, Denvers. I guess Uncle Caesar's been doing it ever since Dad died ten years ago. I've tried to make

168

him quit, but what could I do? First it was cattle, rustling them from spreads on the mainland and running them across the channel at neap tide. They'd put them aboard a two-master Captain García had waiting off Mocha Point, and, by the time Sheriff Giddings got across with his posse, the only cattle on the island would be our own. Now, since the bottom dropped out of the beef market and this Skinning War started, it's been the same with hides." She stopped suddenly, anger pouting her full underlip. "I don't see what cause you have to be so finicky anyway."

It caused him pain to raise his head. "Hardwycke?"

"What's rustling compared to killing a man?" she said. "You're lucky Uncle Caesar let you stay. If you'd tried to get through the posses Giddings will have thrown along the coast, you'd be hanging from a cypress tree right now."

"You think I killed Hardwycke?" he said.

"You must have wanted that twelve hundred dollars pretty bad," she said bitterly, "to murder a man for it."

He shook his head dully. "Listen, I've kept my mouth shut because I didn't know where I stood here. The whole business is getting crazier all the time. I don't even know why I should tell you. How do I know you're not in this with your uncle, just as deep as the others?"

Her breath came heavily. "I'm not, I tell you. If I had any way to stop it, I would. But I can't turn in my own uncle to Giddings. I've tried. More than once, I've tried. But at the last moment I couldn't. It just isn't in me, that's all."

He waved a hand jerkily. "I'll take your word. Will you take mine?"

"For what?"

169

"That I didn't kill Jale Hardwycke," he said. "Bud Richie and I were driving a bunch of steers down from New Mexico to ship at Indianola. We were bedding down that night when we heard the shot. We came across somebody bending over Hardwycke's body there on the Karankawa Trail. The man jumped up and ran away into the brush. The wallet was still sticking out of Hardwycke's hip pocket. I guess we scared the other man away before he'd gotten it. Richie took the wallet out to see if we could identify the dead one. Giddings and his deputies showed up at that moment. I guess they'd been prowling the bayous for your uncle and heard the shot, same as us."

The girl was looking at him intently, and her voice sounded husky. "I want to believe you, Denvers . . . somehow."

He felt sick again and put his head into his hands. The back of his neck was wet, and he saw the china bowl of dirty warm water on the table. The rag beside it showed some blood. Sheridan had really done a job, beating his head against that cypress then. Denvers became aware that the girl had moved closer, and he looked up. There was a strange, taut look in her face that drew him to his feet.

"I've got to believe you," she said. "You're the only one left."

"What do you mean?"

"Uncle Sheridan, Judah, Carnicero. I can't turn to them, can I? Uncle Sheridan's the one who's kept me on the island. When Sinton Navarra came, I thought, maybe, because he was an outsider"—she turned to one side, shrugging—"but he wasn't any help. He's mixed up in it, somehow. Denvers, please stay. . . ."

"Mixed up in what?" said Denvers.

Lamplight caught in her dark hair, with the vague, frustrated shake of her head, and she crossed her arms to rub her shoulders, as if she were cold. "I don't know, really. I can't name it. Something that's been going on here. Not the rustling. . . ."

"Lafitte's ghost?"

She turned on him contemptuously.

"Carnicero said he saw the ghost last night," said Denvers. "It's sort of a legend here? Your father. . . ."

"Arno Sheridan wasn't killed by a ghost," she said angrily. "Whatever killed him was human. My father was found stabbed to death farther up on the island when I was nine years old. I'm not talking about that, anyway. The Lafitte legend was here long before I came. This is something different. Something recent. Maybe you saw it. Between Sinton and Uncle Caesar. Between all the men. They've changed. Watching for something. Waiting."

"You sure it doesn't have to do with this Lafitte business?" he asked. "What's the story?"

"About Lafitte?" She shrugged, turning to look out the window. "He was supposed to have built this house. Called it his Maison Rouge. French, for Red House. The real Maison Rouge was at Galveston Island. Lafitte settled on Galveston after the United States chased him out of Barataria. Then the Americans made him give up Galveston about Eighteen Twenty-One. Nobody really knows what happened to him after that. In fact, nobody really knows anything about the man. He's one of the greatest mysteries of the Gulf, I guess. Most of the stories about him are just legends. This house is certainly old enough to have been built by him. We found some old-fashioned clothes in a chest out in the cypress grove. There's even a story about treasure he

171

buried here on the island. But if you believed the legends, you'd be hunting buried treasure on every island off the Gulf Coast from Padre Island to Gran Terre."

"How about this one?"

She pulled aside the heavy crimson portière, and the open shutter rattled in the wind, and she stared absently outside. "Oh, on his last raid off Matagorda, Lafitte was supposed to have taken a Spanish ship, the *Consolada*, I think, down Cuba way. Half a million in doubloons and gold plate and all the other fixings you hear in one of those pirate stories. He brought it back here and buried it somewhere. You know his old custom of killing the two men he took out to help him dig the hole, so he'd be the only one left who knew its whereabouts? Then his mulatto mistress murdered him in a fit of jealousy, and Lafitte's men left Matagorda without having found the treasure. However, so the story goes, a letter had been written by Jean to his brother, Pierre, telling where this treasure was hidden on Matagorda. Such a letter, of course, would have to be carried by a man Lafitte could trust implicitly, so the tale chooses Dominique, his one-eyed gunner who had fought with Napoleon."

"You sound skeptical," said Denvers.

She shrugged. "I've lived here all my life, Denvers. It's no fairy-tale pirate island spilling over with gold doubloons. It's just a bleak, lonely, empty sandspit, seventy miles long and five miles wide, full of squawking birds and crazy jackrabbits and crazy men."

She whirled away, dropping the portière, pacing restlessly toward the door, and he smiled. "You sound fed up."

She was facing him again, and the sudden, intense bitterness in her voice was startling. "Fed up? I'm going

172

crazy, Denvers. Don't you think I want to get off? I'd give my soul. The farthest inland I've ever been was Refugio and that was when I ran away. Uncle Sheridan found me there and brought me back. Even when I do manage to sneak away, about all I can do is wade across from Dagger Point and get my feet muddy in the swamps. What would I do if I went any farther? Ask someone to let me poke their cattle? I'm not a man. What chance has a girl got? Uncle knows that. He doesn't even bother keeping a very close watch on me. A girl can't run away from home like a boy. Nobody outside would give me a job. I've been in prison all my life. I've never seen the outside world. You don't know how I envy you." She had come toward him again, and he realized how near she was standing and how uncomfortable it made him. "And it isn't just that I'm fed up with the island, Denvers. I'm afraid. This last year, you don't know how I've been afraid. Something's happening here, Denvers. Something evil. . . ."

He stretched out an arm to express his concern. "Wait a minute, Esther. . . ."

"No." She stood rigidly now, looking down at him with a pale, strained face. "I'm not crazy, Denvers. You know it. You felt it when you first entered the house. I saw your face. I saw the way you looked around. It's something you feel and can't see. Tell me you didn't feel it?"

He frowned, mouth tightening. "Maybe I did. I thought it was because I was a stranger, maybe, coming in on this place, or because the house was so old."

She shook her head. "More than that. Something between Sinton and Uncle Sheridan. Something between all the men."

"Just who is Sinton Navarra?" he asked.

173

"The son of Esther's mother," said Sinton Navarra, "by her first husband," and closed the door as he came into the room. His black boots made no sound across the faded nap of the Empire Aubusson, and he moved with that light, swinging ease, so unfitting for such a large man, and his pouched eyes held that veiled inquisition, and a secretive smile played about his lips. "Yes," said Navarra. "Esther's mother had married before she came to Matagorda. Arno Sheridan was her second husband. Her first was Olivier Navarra, my father, who died of malaria at New Orleans in Eighteen Forty-Nine. I was sent to France to be reared and, while there, my mother married again. Thus, while I am really Esther's half-brother, I had not seen her until I came to Matagorda a few months ago. I take it my sister has been telling you of the horrible evil which hangs over this house. Ah. . . ." He held up a pale, long-fingered hand as the girl started to protest. "I understand, my dear, I understand. Matagorda has just gotten on your nerves, that's all. The incessant screaming of those beastly gulls. The never-ceasing pound of the surf." He cocked his dark head, moving to pull the portières aside. "You can hear it now, eh? You can always hear it. Beating, beating, beating, like some diabolical drum, calculated to drive a person insane. No, Esther, I don't blame you. I suppose she gave you the history of the house, too, Denvers." Navarra moved to the scarred Pembroke table at one side of the window, caressing a heavy, tarnished candelabra there. "She doesn't believe Lafitte built this house."

"I never said that," pouted Esther. "I just say you can hear legends about him almost anywhere along the Gulf and very few of them own a shred of truth."

"Perhaps I am more of a romanticist," smiled Navarra

174

softly. "The clothes you found in that old trunk in the garden, for instance, Esther. Or even the furnishings here. If a Colonial had furnished the house, everything would have been matched, don't you think? I mean Chippendale, or Georgian, or Late Empire. But look around you. The bed? French State, I'd say. And this candelabra? Undoubtedly of Spanish origin. And this Pembroke table. Hardly fitting together in one room. My room's the same. A hodgepodge of Louis the Fourteenth and Spanish Colonial and Chippendale."

"You seem to know," said Denvers.

Navarra's shrug was deprecating. "I dealt in furniture in New Orleans for some years."

"I thought it was France?"

Navarra's heavy eyelids flickered with annoyance. "I have been many places, Mister Denvers. Many places."

"From New Orleans you should be an authority on Lafitte."

Navarra seemed to draw himself up. "An authority? I know every move Jean Lafitte made from the time he was born to the time he died, Denvers. I have been separating fact from fancy about Lafitte all my life. I know more about him than. . . ." He stopped abruptly, looking down strangely at Denvers, his brows raising as if in surprise. Then that soft, secretive smile caught at his lips, and he waved a hand. "But that is neither here nor there, is it? After all, Lafitte is long dead, and. . . ."

The scream came through the open shutter, above the sound of the surf, and Navarra was the one to jump for the door after the first stunned surprise had held them all there. "That wasn't any gull!" he said and took the stairs three at a time, stumbling across the dancing steps of the elliptical landing. Early dusk cast a dim luminescence through the circular fanlight above the door, limning a

175

weird, shadowy form darting through the hallway. Denvers rose dizzily from the bed, and Esther rushed to help him keep his balance, while below Navarra tore open the front door and clattered across the pedimented porch. A few stunted cypresses surrounded the house, and Navarra thought he saw a form darting through them. He ran into the trees, taking a flagstoned walk, and stumbled across something, going to his knees. It was a man stretched out on the stones. He caught at Navarra's leg feebly. "I found where he stays," he gasped. "Just like Arno Sheridan I was up past Dagger Point and I found . . . where . . . he stays."

The man had stopped talking by the time Denvers and Esther reached him. Navarra shook him without response. Esther looked at Navarra. "Who is he?"

Navarra toed the dead body with an immaculate boot. "One of Sheridan's hands."

Carnicero came running through the trees, sobbing. "I saw it. *Madre de Dios*. I saw it. Lafitte!"

"Oh, now, Carnicero," said Navarra, raising his hand.

"You don't believe me?" blubbered Carnicero. He bent toward the dead man, pointing a shaking finger at the bloody wound in his side. "Look. Stabbed. The same as Esther's father was stabbed. Not by a knife, *señores y señorita*. Don't you think I've seen enough knife wounds to know? This man was stabbed by a sword!"

## V

THE STENCH OF ROTTEN MEAT WAS SO STRONG IT HAD begun to nauseate Ernie Denvers. The only sound for a long time had been the squealing birds and the dull pound of the surf. *No wonder the girl was fed up*, he thought. *Fed up? A man could go mad in a place like*

176

*this*. He sat heavily on the paint mare they had given him, slitting his eyes against the biting sand blown up by the morning Gulf wind. Ahead was Mocha Point, a long, rickety pier jutting out from the high spit of grass-topped land, and all along the shore were huge piles of decaying beef, covered black with scavenging birds.

"All legal," Caesar Sheridan was saying. "Nothing wrong with having our own packery on Matagorda, see? Shank Pierce has one across the bay. That's where most of the cows in Texas are going now. Private packing. Hides and tallow. And who can stop us from packing our own tallow and skinning our own beef here? Nobody. We run our herds on the island, don't we?"

"And if you wade across to the mainland every night after a few dozen of somebody else's hides, who's to know the difference?" said Denvers sarcastically.

Sheridan threw back his head to let out that roaring laugh. "That's right, boy, that's right. A fallen hide belongs to anyone who wants to skin it, no matter what the brand. Just like in the old days a maverick belonged to anybody who put his dally on it. That's the law. And that's the Skinning War. Texas is full of hide rustlers that help a hide to fall by filling it full of holes. That's why Giddings can't prove anything on us. All he's ever seen is the carcasses we leave. Could be any one of half a dozen gangs operating along the coast. Time Sheriff Giddings gets over here, our shipment of hides has left aboard the two-master García docks here to load up, brands blotted out and everything."

Navarra had a silk handkerchief held across his nose. "That Mexican who was killed yesterday smelled almost as foul as this, Caesar. Was he one of the hands you have down here?"

Sheridan nodded. "This Lafitte thing is getting on my

177

nerves. Any more trouble like that and my Mexicans are going to leave the island."

"Have you ever seen this ghost yourself?" asked Denvers.

Navarra waved his handkerchief disgustedly. "Of course he hasn't. These Mexicans are just a bunch of superstitious animals."

"Why would it necessarily have to be Lafitte's *ghost?*" asked Denvers. "You can laugh off Carnicero's stories, but not that dead Mexican a week ago. Killed with a sword? Who carries a sword nowadays?"

Sheridan frowned at him. "Don't be loco. Those Lafitte stories are so much tripe."

"Navarra doesn't really think so," said Denvers. "When was Lafitte supposed to have died, Navarra?"

"*Supposed?*" Navarra's voice was sharp. "He did die. You know the story."

"And a hundred others," said Sheridan. "I've hit just about every town along the Gulf, from Port Isabel to New Orleans, and every one has Lafitte dying in their own town hall. I met an old sea captain at San Antone who claimed he saw Lafitte on his death bed there in Eighteen Thirty-One. I saw another one who swore he found Lafitte's grave near Indianola."

"He died in Eighteen Twenty-Six," said Navarra angrily. "He was in his middle thirties."

"And this is Eighteen Seventy-Five," mused Denvers. "Fifty years added to a man's middle thirties. Have you ever seen all of Matagorda Island, Sheridan?"

The older man shrugged. "No need to. Nothing up at the other end. We run cattle down here. Island's too big to use all of it."

"This is fantastic," said Navarra. "Lafitte was a brilliant man, a vivid cosmopolitan, a gentleman of the

178

world. Even supposing he didn't die, a man like that wouldn't isolate himself on a lonely. . . ."

"You said yourself this place could drive a man mad, Navarra," grinned Denvers.

"But fifty years . . . ?"

"I've seen a lot of spry old men past eighty."

Navarra turned away, swabbing angrily at his nose with the handkerchief. "I refuse to discuss it any longer."

Sheridan leaned back in his saddle, slapping his thigh with a raucous laugh. "He's gotcha, Sinton. That dead Mexican didn't meet up with no ghost and neither did my brother. How do you know Denvers ain't right? Maybe that story about Lafitte building this house is true. Maybe the old boy's been running around here with his sword like Carnicero claims."

"Don't be a stupid ass," said Navarra thinly.

Sheridan's laugh broke off abruptly, and he spurred his horse, jumping it around in front of Denvers's paint to bring the animal broadside across the head of Navarra's black. He grabbed the black's bridle, yanking it around till he held its head down by the rump of his horse and was facing Navarra. "Don't call me names, Sinton," he said.

All the indignant hauteur had slipped from Navarra, and his smooth, soft voice formed a sharp contrast against Sheridan's guttural roar. "Take your hands off my bridle. I don't like it."

"Maybe we better make it clear who bosses this island before I do that, Sinton," said Sheridan.

"Caesar," said Navarra deliberately, "don't threaten me. I'm not one of your Mexican hands. I'm not afraid of you."

Sheridan looked at Navarra a long moment. "No," he

179

said finally. "No, I don't think you are, Sinton. But get this"—he yanked viciously upward on the bridle, causing the black to jump—"I'm running Matagorda and, nephew or no nephew, you'll do as I say when you're here. You've been bucking me ever since you came, Sinton. I don't know what it is. I can't put my hands on it, but it's been there. Don't go any further." He jerked the bridle again. "Don't let me get my hands on it. If you do, I'll tear it apart and you, too."

He threw the horse's head away from him and necked his own fat bay around, flapping both feet out wide to bring them in with a solid, popping sound, and the bay jumped forward. Navarra sat his black there without moving, watching Sheridan go. There was an ineffable evil in the way his thick lids had closed almost shut over his eyes, the network of minute veins giving the pouched, dissolute flesh a sickly blue shadow. He seemed to become aware that Denvers was watching him and turned, glancing at him momentarily. Then, with an angry thrust of his head, he urged his horse forward.

There was a row of tallow vats along the shore near the pier and back of them was the slaughter shanty. Prieto and another Mexican were skinning carcasses by the shanty, and Carnicero was mounting a bloody-hoofed horse preparatory to hauling a skinned cow to the nearest pile of rotting meat.

"We tried salting the beef," Sheridan told Denvers. "But all we could get for a two-hundred-pound barrel was nine dollars. Even that tallow don't bring much more than what it costs to ship. The hides are the only things that really pay. You help Prieto with the skinning today."

Carnicero disappeared behind the piles of meat,

180

hauling his carcass, and came back to dismount and climb up a ladder on the nearest tallow vat. Denvers was off his paint by then, rolling up his sleeves, when the Mexican *vaquero* came fogging through the piles of carcasses, his sombrero flapping against his back. "Another cut of steers disappeared from our north herd this morning," he called to Sheridan, hauling his lathered horse to a stop.

"Did you see anything?"

The man crossed himself. "*Madre de Dios*, does one see an *espiritu!*"

Sheridan turned to Navarra, face turning dark. "There's your ghost again. How do you explain that?"

"I don't purport to," said Navarra. "I just say Lafitte died in Eighteen Twenty-Six."

"Hell!" snarled Sheridan, turning to Prieto. "I'm going out to see what kind of tracks they found this time. You put Denvers to work."

The odor of rotting meat was oppressive, and Denvers reached for his bandanna to slip it over his nose. It was then he noticed how Prieto was watching him. The man's thin, bitter face was turned after Sheridan, riding away, but his glittering black eyes were looking sideways toward Denvers, and they held a sly, waiting light that stopped Denvers's hand with the bandanna just beneath his jaw. Then he heard the squeak of saddle leather behind him. Navarra?

"Did someone really cut out a bunch of steers this morning?" said Navarra.

"Strangely enough, yes," said Prieto, turning fully around toward Denvers, smiling mirthlessly. "I heard about it before sunup and sent word to have someone ride in with the news when Caesar came. If it hadn't happened that way, I would have found something else

181

to pull him away."

Denvers caught his first sight of Judah coming down between the piles of beef, slapping at the swarm of flies buzzing around his great, black, sweating torso. He had a big meat cleaver in one hand.

"Good," said Navarra from behind Denvers. "Good."

Carnicero was now climbing down the ladder from the top of the tallow vat and moving with heavy feet toward Denvers from the opposite side of Judah. Denvers couldn't keep his eye on all of them at the same time.

"We've been wanting to get you alone like this," said Navarra.

"You mean you don't want Sheridan to know?" said Denvers, and his voice sounded like mesquite scratching saddle leather.

"You might put it that way," said Navarra, taking a small step around in front of Denvers. "I think you know what we want, Denvers."

Denvers had never wanted a gun so desperately. Four of them. Three on the mainland had been bad enough, and even there with his gun he had gone into it knowing how it would end. But now four. "This is why you didn't let Sheriff Giddings take me?" he said tensely. "What's in Hardwycke's wallet you all want so bad?"

"Surely you know," said Navarra.

"Not the twelve hundred dollars."

"Not the twelve hundred dollars," said Navarra.

"Maybe I don't have the wallet."

Navarra's blue-shadowed lids closed slowly across his black eyes. "I think you have. You can give it to us now. Or we can take it. Whichever way you prefer."

*Whichever way you prefer*. It almost made Denvers laugh. Whichever way you prefer. Sheridan wouldn't be coming back this time. All right. He still felt weak from the last fight but what the hell. He spread his feet a little in the sand.

"Am I to assume that you wish us to take it?" said Navarra.

"I can't give you what I don't have."

Carnicero had his *saca de tripas* out. That wasn't so much. Neither was Judah's cleaver. It was the gun. He wouldn't stand a chance after one of them pulled a gun. He couldn't let it get that far. All right. That would start it then. The first man to go for his gun would start it. He was still watching Navarra and remembering that French Le Page in the man's shoulder harness.

"If you don't have it on your person," said Navarra, "we'll find out where you put it."

"You won't lay a hand on me."

"We'll find out where you put it. If you don't have it on you. Either way. It doesn't matter. Once more, Denvers. Will you give us the wallet?"

The surf boomed dismally behind Denvers, and the gulls swarming over the rotten piles of meat made a horrible, raucous din, and the sweat had soaked through his shirt beneath the armpits. *The first man to go for his iron.* Judah's bare feet made a shuffling sound in the sand. Denvers ran his tongue across dry lips. The first man.

"Why waste time?" snarled Prieto.

"All right," said Navarra, and it was he.

There was no thought behind Denvers's move. He had been so keyed up to it that he felt nothing, actually, until he struck Navarra. He must have leaped, because he heard his own grunt, and then he was up against the big, dark man, grabbing for the hand Navarra had snaked behind his coat, and all of them were shouting

183

around him. Denvers's weight carried Navarra backward, and the two of them reeled across the sand, knocking Prieto aside as he sought to draw his gun. For that moment surprise robbed Navarra of any reaction. By the time he had recovered, Denvers had the man's hand twisted around, jerking the big French pin-fire from it. Still staggering backward to keep from falling, Navarra floundered into the surf and, with the first wet slap of brine against his legs, Denvers responded to the drive of a heavy body crashing onto his back.

"No, Judah, don't," screamed Navarra, tearing free of Denvers. "You'll kill him."

The blow that struck Denvers's head sent him to his knees with the Le Page still gripped desperately in his fist. Through the roaring pain in him he sensed that the giant mulatto was shifting to strike again and rolled sideways through the shallow water, trying to keep the gun held above it. Navarra tried to catch him and got one hand on his shoulder. In that moment Denvers felt the violence of the man's strength. Then he had torn free, with Judah's meat axe slapping the water where he had been a moment before. Still floundering away, he realized the mulatto must have been set to cleave him in two and had shifted the axe in the last moment to strike with the flat of the blade instead of the edge, when Navarra had first shouted.

Prieto's shot sounded sharply above the dull wash of the surf, and Denvers whirled toward him, struggling to his feet. Still stunned by the mulatto's blow, he was surprised to feel the French gun jump in his hand, and the explosion jarred him partly out of his dazed pain. He heard Prieto's shout, and Prieto's gun go off again, and the lead splashed water up at him, and then he had the Le Page going. It sounded like a whole crew of

184

triggermen fanning their irons in front of his face, and he had never dreamed a gun could sling so much lead.

"Navarra," he heard Prieto yell, "stop him," and then Prieto stopped yelling and, knowing that was over, Denvers whirled to meet Judah as the mulatto floundered through the water toward him with the meat cleaver. Denvers's shot went into the foaming breaker at his feet, and he followed it, driven down by the man who had leaped on his back. He twisted around, firing blindly against the man's body, but the gun had been in the water now, and it made a soggy, clicking sound. Desperately he pistol-whipped the contorted face above him. Carnicero? It was gone, and he heard the man's pained cries, and he was trying to get to his feet again, gasping and choking, spitting out salt water, when he caught the flash of Judah's cleaver.

His plunge aside ducked his head beneath the sea again, and he threw himself at Judah, blinded by the stinging brine, feeling Judah's arm strike his shoulder with the blow that had missed. Inside the reach of that cleaver now, he struck at Judah's face with the gun. He heard the mulatto's hoarse scream and followed the falling body on back, straddling it to strike again, driving the man's bloody face beneath the water. The next breaker washed Denvers off Judah's limp frame, and he floundered backward, off balance, into Navarra who had been stumbling toward him from the shallow water.

Waist deep they met, and Navarra's hands caught Denvers's wrist as Denvers tried to strike with the Le Page. They reeled back and forth with the breakers carrying them inshore and the backwash carrying them out again, Navarra trying to twist Denvers's arm around so he couldn't use the gun. Finally the heavy man

185

twisted Denvers into position to apply pressure, and the pain brought a strangled shout from Denvers, and he felt the gun slip from his fingers, falling into the water. He tore his wrist free of Navarra's grasp, seeking the man's legs beneath the water. He found them and snaked one foot behind Navarra's knee, suddenly throwing his whole weight against the man.

Navarra stumbled backward, and at that moment a breaker struck them, carrying the larger man down with Denvers on top. It washed their struggling bodies inshore until Denvers was straddling Navarra in shallow water, his knees on the sandy bottom, his head above the sea. He found Navarra's neck with both hands and held the man's head down that way, feeling the thick muscles swell and writhe beneath his fingers as Navarra tried to rise above the water. Another roller foamed over, and Denvers's own head was submerged. When it had passed, he came out gasping and coughing, still holding the other man under with a desperate grip. Navarra jerked back and forth beneath Denvers in a spasmodic frenzy, hands clawing, legs kicking, but his struggles were growing weaker. A man was on Denvers's back then, tearing him off Navarra. He twisted from one side to the other under the blows, clinging with the last of his strength to the man beneath him.

"¡Por Dios!" shouted the one on his back, hooking an arm around his neck. "He's dead now. Get off him, will you? I keel you!"

Navarra's struggles ceased, and Denvers released his hold, turning to thrust feebly at Carnicero. The Mexican had one arm around Denvers's neck, the other drawn back with his knife. Denvers tugged weakly to one side, and they rolled off Navarra. A breaker swept them up

186

on the wet sand at the water's edge. Carnicero rose above Denvers, straddling him. Denvers tried to catch the knife arm, but the whole desperate struggle had left no strength in him, and his grab missed, and his breath left him in a weary gust. Carnicero held the knife suspended above Denvers's chest for a long moment, a strange, indefinable expression crossing his face. Then the first lugubrious tear dropped from his eye.

"I can't," he said, and the tears began to stream down his face. "I was born with a *saca de tripas* in my hand. They pinned my swaddling clothes together with stilettos. I ate my *frijoles* with a Bowie knife from the time I was two. All my life they have called me Butcher for what I can do with a knife. And now, when I get the chance"—he began to whimper like a baby—"I can't keel you!"

## VI

SOMEWHERE IN AN UPSTAIRS ROOM A SHUTTER slapped dismally in the wind. The chamber they had given Denvers was dark, and a rotten board creaked every time he paced past the Pembroke table. He halted at the window a moment, drawing aside the tawdry portières of crimson damask to look out at the somber clouds scudding across the slate-colored afternoon sky. He was hungry, and his boots were still soggy from the fight in the surf, and his head throbbed painfully from the blow Judah had given him with the flat of the meat cleaver. He turned back to start pacing restlessly again and then stopped abruptly, hearing the rattle of the door. Esther Sheridan pushed it open hesitantly and came in with a candle.

"It's getting dark," she said. "I thought you might like

a lamp."

He watched her lift the glass reservoir on the Sandwich lamp, adjusting the wick spout until the candle flame caught. The camphine sent out a pungent odor, and the flickering light rose to glow against the curve of her cheek before she settled the glass again. Then she blew out the candle and stuck it in an empty socket of the candelabra on the Pembroke. It brought her close to him and, when she turned, there was a searching depth to her eyes. "What is it they have against you, Denvers?"

"Who?"

"Prieto's pretty badly wounded," she muttered, still studying his face. "They don't think he'll live. Navarra must have been pretty nearly drowned. He's still in his bed. Judah's face looks like a side of beef somebody's been chopping steaks off of. Or maybe it's not what they have against you. Maybe it's what they want from you."

He turned away from her, going shakily to the window again, wondering if he still feared that he couldn't trust her, or if it were himself he couldn't trust now. It did something inside him to have her stand that close. Esther was only nineteen, and yet she did something inside him. He couldn't smell the camphine any more. He wondered what made her hair so sweet.

The girl began to laugh suddenly. "I guess they didn't know what kind of *cimarrón* they were stringing their dallies on when they jumped you. Four at once and you haven't even got a scratch on you to show for it!"

"My head hurts, my body aches everywhere, and I have trouble standing up," he said and shifted uncomfortably as he sensed her beside him again.

"What is it?" she asked insistently.

188

He turned suddenly, driven somehow by her nearness, by the scent of her black hair, wanting to trust someone. "The wallet, the wallet. What else?"

She drew a sharp breath. "Hardwycke's wallet?"

"Navarra started to ask me for it when I first got here," said Denvers. "Changed his mind when your uncle came into the room. I didn't even realize Navarra had asked me for it. Then Prieto began putting on the screws when we went after those hides on the mainland night before last. Your uncle broke that up again. Yesterday afternoon they got Caesar away for good."

"They're afraid of him," she said.

"Navarra isn't," said Denvers.

"I don't think Sinton Navarra is afraid of anything," she muttered. "But the others are afraid of Uncle Caesar. You saw what he did to you. You can lick all four of them put together, but you can't lick Uncle Caesar. Do you blame them for fearing him? I'm afraid of him myself."

"Maybe they do fear him," he said, "but is that the reason they wanted him gone?"

"If Sinton's up to something, Uncle Caesar would kill him, if he found out. What's in the wallet they want so badly?"

He shrugged. "How should I know? I don't have it."

Her voice was surprised. "Who does?"

"Sheriff Giddings," said Denvers. "He took it from Bud Richie."

"But you took his horse, he said."

Denvers jerked his dark head impatiently. "Giddings followed me here, didn't he?"

She caught at his arm. "But that doesn't mean he found where his horse had dropped beneath you, Denvers. I found you in that cane brake opening onto

189

the sea. How far back had you left the dead horse?"

"At the head of the bayou," he said. "Beyond those canes."

Her voice was rising now. "That's Indian Bog. You must have come through the bog itself. Nobody takes that route. It's too dangerous. We've lost more cattle in there than any other bayou on this coast."

"I found a solid strip in the muck," he said. "They were right on my heels, and I had to take a chance."

"But Giddings wouldn't have followed you that way. It's the only reason you gave him the slip. He'd take the edge of the bog around to the coast before crossing at Dagger Point. And if he came that way, he'd never find his dead horse."

"If the wallet's still there. . . ."

"It might tell us what this is all about," she cried. "Listen. We can't leave the house together. Uncle Caesar thinks we're trapped here because the tide's in, and there aren't any boats on this side. He won't be watching so closely. When they all go back into the kitchen to eat, slip out the side door and meet me in the cypress grove."

## VII

CAESAR SHERIDAN WAS SITTING AT THE BIG OAK TABLE in the living room, playing solitaire, and he grunted as Denvers entered. "You seen Sinton?"

"Navarra? Not since yesterday."

"He ain't in his room," said Sheridan, slapping a queen down disgustedly. Then he turned in his chair, putting a beefy hand on his knee. "What happened yesterday, anyway? What's between you and Navarra?"

"Maybe he doesn't like the way I part my hair," said

190

Denvers.

Sheridan snorted like a ringy bull. "Don't try to put that in my Stetson. Ever since Sinton hit this island, there's been something funny going on. You in it?" Denvers started to answer, but Sheridan went on, turning back to the cards, talking more to himself than to Denvers. "When Sinton first showed up, I let him stay because he was kinfolk. Now I'm afraid to let him go for fear the sheriff will tie onto him, and Sinton will talk. Same reason I'm afraid to let you go. You ain't planning a run-out, are you? I'll bet. Well, it won't do no good. Tide's in now, and you'll get pulled down by the rip if you try to swim. I've got a Mexican down at the barn with orders to shoot, if you try to sneak a horse. I swear, Denvers, I don't know what to do with you. Messing up my men. Bringing the sheriff down on my head. Up to something, I swear. . . ."

"Beans on," said Judah from the kitchen door. He stood there, looking at Denvers with murder in his eyes as black as the hide on his bruised, lacerated face. Sheridan shoved his chair back and rose with a grunt. "Coming?"

"I'm not hungry," said Denvers.

Sheridan threw back his head to laugh "You mean you don't hanker to go in Judah's kitchen and let him hang over you with a butcher knife. Well, I can't say as I blame you. One time's enough for a while."

He stomped through the kitchen door, growling something at the mulatto. After a moment Denvers moved across the parlor to the side door. It was unlocked, and he slipped out. The cypresses acquiesced to the biting wind with a mournful sigh, heavy foliage beating into Denvers's face as he sought the girl. She startled him by stepping from behind a huge trunk.

191

Without a word she led him over the short, rank prairie grass that covered the inland portion of the island, reaching the sandy shore finally. The moon had risen by then, and Denvers took off his high-heeled boots to walk the rest of the way. It took them an hour to reach the spot past Dagger Point where the tall sea grass flanked a bayou that cut back into the island. His feet sank ankle deep into the muck as he dropped down its bank toward the water. Finally the girl parted the growth from the prow of a skiff.

"Uncle doesn't know about this," said Esther. "I came across it last year, hidden up here. Somebody else must have been using it. I've found new pitch in the seams several times."

He helped her haul the leaky, battered skiff into the water. "Anybody else on the island?"

"Some Mexicans on the other end, but that's fifty-six miles. Maybe a few crazy hermits in between. Uncle says you always find them on a place like this. We had a couple helping us brand last fall. Maybe one of them."

He had never rowed a boat before, and they made heavy work of it across the choppy channel. About half way over they had shipped so much water that Esther had to bail with his hat while he worked the splintery oars. They reached the shore of the mainland and hunted along the coast until long after midnight before finding the mouth of the bayou leading toward Indian Bog. Finally the reeds and muck of the bayou became too thick for further rowing, and they hauled the boat ashore, hiding it in some salt grass. The air here was oppressive with the scent of hyacinth growing along the water, and the festoons of Spanish moss caught wetly at Denvers's shoulders as Esther led him inland. Stumbling wearily through the tangled marshes, tormented by the vicious mosquitoes, they at last found the pipestem brake Denvers had broken through that night and hesitantly penetrated the rattling canes. The booming of the frogs rose all about them, and somewhere a panther squalled. Esther's hand was suddenly thrust into his, warm and moist, and her voice sounded strained. "You'll have to lead the way from here on in. Think you can remember?"

The bellow of a 'gator startled him. He parted the canes with his free hand, peering into the gloom ahead, hunting for that big spread of water lilies he had stumbled through. Then his foot sank into rotten mud up to his knee, and the girl caught at him with a sharp cry. Indian Bog? Indian Bog. On the right he caught the sickly white gleam of lilies. There was something revolting about the whole place. The canes rattled like hollow bones, and the salt grass stank, and a foul odor of decay rose from the mud, and the wild hyacinth waved feebly in the breeze like dying hands. The first sign they had of the horse was the buzz of flies. The moon was sinking with the coming morning, and they barely made out the rotting carcass, covered with flies and gnats, half eaten away by scavengers. Stomach knotting, Denvers forced himself to approach the animal. The Mexican saddlebags Giddings had carried were called *alforjas*, and, when Denvers bent to open them, the flies swarmed up with a loud, angry buzzing, sending a revulsion through him so sharp he almost jumped back. He ripped at the pocket of the *alforjas* and put his hand inside.

"All right," said a soft voice from behind him. "Pull it out and give it to me."

Denvers took his hand slowly from the saddlebags, turning to face Navarra who stood in the cane brake.

193

The man had recovered his Le Page from the surf the day before, and it was in his hand now. Behind him Carnicero's bucolic face showed dimly in the darkness. The girl stood where Denvers had left her, a taut surprise on her face, her hands to her mouth.

"We came across at low tide," smiled Navarra. "Been hunting up and down the coast for that dead horse all evening. Thought maybe you'd been telling the truth about not having the wallet. Then Carnicero spotted you coming down the shore in that skiff. We followed you in through the bayou, going along the edge. Give the wallet to me, Denvers."

"The *alforjas* are empty," said Denvers.

He saw the little muscles bunch up beneath the thick flesh of Navarra's heavy jaw. With a muttered curse Navarra rushed at him, shoving him aside to stoop over the saddlebags.

"Never mind, Navarra. Denvers is right. The *alforjas* are empty."

Navarra stiffened perceptibly then straightened from the dead animal. Denvers saw him then, Sheriff Giddings, standing on past Esther, his big Colts gleaming dully in his hands. Navarra made a small, spastic gesture to raise his Le Page.

"Don't," said Giddings. "Ollie's behind you. Drop the gun, or you'll be deader'n that hoss." The sheriff began moving forward. "Think we wouldn't figure on this? When I saw Denvers at your house on the island, I couldn't be sure he was my man. Like you say, it was dark that night of Hardwycke's murder, and, even up close, I didn't get a good enough look at him to identify positive. But I knew that bullet I'd put in my hoss would drop him eventually. Took us a long time to find the animal. Think you'd reach it before we did, Denvers?

194

When I found that wallet still in the saddlebags. . . ."

"You have the wallet?" Navarra asked.

Sheriff Giddings answered sharply. "That's right. You won't get the twelve hundred dollars, either. I been hunting thieves half my life, Navarra, and I know the way their minds work. Like I say, when I found that wallet still in the saddlebags, I knew Denvers would be back. I knew just how his mind would work. It was that twelve hundred dollars he killed Hardwycke for, and it would draw him back like a fly to molasses. Soon's he discovered he'd left it on the hoss, he'd be coming. So I just squatted with my posse. Looks like I got a bigger catch than I planned. That's all right, too. There's a little matter of some Pothook steers I'd like to discuss with you. It's getting near dawn now. Ollie, you get the horses, and we'll take these folks to Refugio."

Ollie Minster made a short, squat shadow back in the canes, moving to get the horses. Denvers saw the shift of other possemen. Two of them were closing in from behind a cypress, holding carbines. Denvers was half turned toward Carnicero when he saw the Mexican staring past the two men who had just appeared from behind the tree. He raised his hand to point, and his voice was hardly audible.

"*Madre de Dios*. There it is. Believe me now? See for yourself. *Madre de Dios*. Jean Lafitte himself!"

Denvers didn't actually see anything beyond the two men except that first shadowy movement in the trees, and then they turned with their guns. One of them shouted hoarsely, and the Spanish moss whipped around them with their scuffle. Then the man who had shouted staggered backward, gasping. The other began pumping his gun.

"Giddings," he shouted, and his voice was drowned

195

by his racketing Winchester, "I saw him, Giddings. Damn my eyes if I didn't. I saw him!"

"John," shouted Giddings, whirling that way. "Stop, you fool. Carterwright! You'll get sucked down in that bog, John. Come back."

The posseman who had staggered backward was crouched down on his knees now, hugging his belly, and Denvers realized he must have been stabbed. The one Giddings had called Carterwright was running into the cypresses, still shouting. Giddings made a small, jerky move after him, shouting again. "John don't," he called and for that moment was turned away from Denvers and Navarra. "Carterwright!"

Denvers jumped toward him, and Navarra bent to scoop up his Le Page. Giddings was whirling back as Denvers's body struck him. They went staggering into the canes, one of the sheriff's six-shooters deafening Denvers with its explosion. Denvers caught the gun between them, feeling it leap hotly beneath his hand as Giddings thumbed the hammer again. Giddings tried to beat at Denvers with the other gun. Denvers ducked the blow, tripping the man. They crashed down into the brake, and Denvers let his body fall dead weight onto Giddings. He heard the man grunt sickly, and for that instant the sheriff's body was limp beneath him. Denvers tore a Colt free from Giddings's hand, struggling to his feet. Navarra came in from behind him before he was fully erect, slugging at him with the Le Page. Denvers rolled aside, getting the blow across his neck instead of on the head. Dazed, he caught at the canes to keep from falling. Navarra bent over Giddings, striking him on the head with the barrel of his pin-fire. Giddings sank back, and Navarra pulled something from the sheriff's pocket. "Carnicero," he shouted. "I've got

196

it. Come on. I've got it."

The Mexican stumbled through the brake from somewhere, panting. Then the sound of horses came to them, and Ollie Minster was shouting. "Giddings, Giddings? Where are you? Giddings?"

"Over in the brake," shouted the one named Carterwright, coming in out of the bog. "Navarra and that other ranny jumped Giddings."

The canes crashed as Minster drove his horse into them. Navarra dove to one side, disappearing in the pipestems, but the horse was on Denvers before he could follow. Then it went through his mind. Just in that instant while the horse was looming up above him big and black. Just the name. The name he had known so long before. All the way down from New Mexico. And the time even before that. Bud Richie. He didn't even try to get out of the way. He lunged for the animal, the shock of striking its chest knocking him aside. Then he had his hand on the stirrup leather, and the horse was dragging him off his feet. He had the Colt he had taken from Giddings, and he had that last moment before he had to let go. "Remember Bud Richie," he screamed up at Ollie Minster, the canes rattling and slamming all around him as he was dragged through them, his foot giving a last kick at solid ground. "Remember Bud Richie?"

Minster twisted on the horse, face ugly and contorted above Denvers, trying to bring his gun around in time. "Don't, Denvers. I didn't. Denvers . . . !"

Denvers's Colt cut him off, crashing just once, and Denvers saw Ollie slide off the opposite side of the horse with the pain stamped into his face. Then Denvers couldn't hang on any longer and let go of the stirrup leather to roll crashing through the pipestems. He came

197

to a stop and lay there, hearing Carterwright call something from behind. He got to his knees finally, shaking his head, and crawled through the canes till he could no longer hear the man. He figured the girl would have made for the boat and tried to take a direction that would lead him to the bayou.

He had found the slippery, mucky bank of the bayou and was stumbling down it toward the sea when the horses crashed through the canes behind him. He whirled, raising the Colt, hammer eared back under his thumb before he saw it wasn't Carterwright. "Ollie was leading the other possemen's horses," cried Esther, throwing him the reins of one of the animals she had been leading. "He let them go to follow you, and I got them."

He caught the reins and threw them back over the head of a big buckskin. The heavy horse wheeled beneath him as he stepped aboard, and he slapped into the saddle with the animal already in its gallop. The other two horses, having been released by Esther, followed Denvers and the girl for a while but soon trailed off and disappeared behind. Dawn was lighting the sky when the two reached Dagger Point, and he saw the two horsemen ahead of them out in the channel.

"Neap tide came while we were on the mainland," called the girl. "It's about time for high tide to come in again. Looks like Navarra's already having trouble. It's suicide, if the rip catches us before we're across. Want to chance it?"

Denvers pointed back of them along the coast. "We'll have to."

The girl took one look at the pair of horsebackers fogging across the shore from the direction of the bayou and turned her own animal into the rollers. Denvers could feel the riptide catch at his buckskin as he followed. He remembered the first time they had waded across here and realized how much deeper it was as the horse sank up to its belly in the first shallows. The animal threw up its head, nickering, and tried to turn back. Denvers bunched up his reins and drove it forward, water slopping in over the tops of his boots suddenly, then reaching to his knees. The undertow swept the buckskin helplessly to one side, and Denvers felt the animal's feet go out from under for an instant.

Esther's horse was a little pinto, maybe two hands shorter than the buckskin, and its head was already under. Fighting it, she turned in her saddle to shout above the growing wind. "Don't let your horse start swimming. The rip will sweep you away from the shallow part as soon as its feet leave bottom, and you'll never be able to touch down again. Hurry up, Denvers, hurry up."

The solid feel was gone from beneath him, and he realized the horse was trying to swim. His reins made a wet, popping sound against its hide as he lashed it and yanked its head viciously from side to side. Long years of habitual reaction to that made the buckskin put its feet down and try to break into a gallop. Ahead the pinto was floundering helplessly, black tail and mane floating on the water. It began slipping to one side, and Denvers heard the girl's frantic cry. He raked his buckskin under water with his spurs, and the frenzied beast heaved forward, whinnying in pain, tossing its head. The pinto was already being swept away by the riptide as it strove to swim, no longer able to touch bottom. Denvers unlashed his dally rope from the buckskin's horn, shaking out several loops and heaving the length to Esther. "You told me yourself," he shouted at her.

"Don't try to fight that pinto. You're off the bar already. Grab my rope before you're out of reach. This buckskin's taller. Maybe he can make it."

Esther jumped from her pinto into the water, grasping desperately at the rope. Coughing, gasping, she pulled herself in. He hooked an arm about her wet, lithe waist, pulling her onto the buckskin behind him. Ahead he saw that Navarra and Carnicero had reached the surf and were climbing onto the island. Denvers raked the buckskin with the rowels again, hearing the horse's nicker above the wind, feeling it surge forward. The undertow kept sweeping at it malignantly, and every time the animal sought to lift its legs and swim, Denvers bunched his reins and yanked its head from side to side. His hands were raw from tugging on the leather, and the brine brought stinging pain to the abrasions. Soggy, dripping, they finally reached the surf, and the buckskin broke into a weary trot, urged on by the rollers at its rump. Navarra had dismounted on the sand dunes, and, when he approached near enough, Denvers saw that the man had a wallet in his hands.

"It was on Giddings," said Navarra, throwing up his head to look at Denvers, voice suddenly ironic. "I suppose I owe you an apology, Denvers."

Still sitting his horse, Carnicero shouted and pointed toward the channel. Sheriff Giddings and Carterwright had driven their horses into the water and were coming across. Denvers didn't realize how strong the wind had grown until the girl screamed. "Go back," she called, and Denvers himself could hardly hear her voice above the whining blow. "Giddings, don't be a fool. High tide's coming in. We barely made it ourselves. You'll be swept off the bar."

She stopped shouting as Carterwright was abruptly

200

turned aside, his horse floundering in the choppy sea a moment, then shooting down the channel. Giddings tried to turn his horse back, but the rip caught it, and a high swell hit him. When the horse showed topping the swell, Giddings was out of the saddle. Esther put her face in her hands, and her shoulders began to shake. Denvers felt sick at his stomach, somehow, and turned away. He became aware that all this time Sinton Navarra had been pawing through the wallet. Money lay scattered all over the sand, and Navarra was tearing the last greenbacks heedlessly from the pocket of the leather case. "It isn't here, Carnicero. It isn't here!" He threw up his head that way suddenly, wind catching at the white streak in his long, black hair, and the wild light in his eyes was turned sly and secretive as his bluish lids drew almost shut over them. "You've got it, Denvers. You had it all along."

"What?"

"You know," Navarra almost screamed, and his suavity was swept away now. "You know what I've wanted all along. That's what you were after when you killed Hardwycke. Not the money. Are you from New Orleans? Give it to me, Denvers. I'll kill you this time, I swear I will."

"That's all, Navarra!"

Navarra had reached for his Le Page, but his whole motion stopped with his hand still beneath his coat. Denvers had stuck Giddings's Colt in his belt, and that was where he had drawn it from.

"I told you he could get it out pretty quick," said the girl, laughing shakily. Then she cast another look out to sea, and a sick horror crossed her face. She caught at Denvers's arm. "Whatever we do now had better be back at the house. This is a real blow coming up."

201

Denvers hardly heard her. "Navarra," he said, "what did you want in that wallet?"

## VIII

THE ANCIENT HOUSE TREMBLED TO THE BLASTING malignancy of the wind, and somewhere on the second story a loose shutter clattered insanely against the warped weatherboards. The cypresses bowed their hoary heads and wept streamers of Spanish moss that were caught up by the storm and swept away like writhing snakes to tangle at Ernie Denvers's feet as he stumbled through the grove, one hand pulling Esther along after him. They hitched their horses to the rack in front of the long, columned porch. Denvers waved the Colt impatiently for Navarra to go ahead. He had taken the Le Page from the man, but had been unable to force Navarra to tell what he had wanted from the wallet. The front door creaked dismally, and Carnicero went in and stopped. Navarra went in and stopped. Denvers saw why as soon as he stepped through the portal. Revealed by the light of a single candle on the table, Judah was crouched over Caesar Sheridan, lying sprawled on the floor. The mulatto was looking at them, and the whites of his eyes gleamed from his black, sweating face.

"It killed Uncle Caesar," whispered Judah, and his voice got louder as he spoke. "It's here in this house. I saw it. My own eyes. I saw it."

Carnicero worked his lips a moment before he could get the words out. "Who?"

"You know who," said Judah. "All dressed up in his satin knee breeches and cocked hat, like he was going to a party. Rings on his fingers and gold buttons on his coat. You know who."

202

"*¡La fantasma!*" choked Carnicero and crossed himself. "Jean Lafitte. . . ."

The laugh stopped him. It came crazy and warped on the howling wind, partly drowned out by the clattering shutter. They all turned to look at the stairs, circling up the dancing steps to the top landing. It was a shadowy form, at first, moving down out of the darkness. The candlelight flickered across the gold buttons on the long, blue tailcoat then caught the gilt *fleur de lys* embroidered across cuffs and collar. Denvers had seen pictures of the dress worn in the early Eighteen hundreds. He recognized the high, Hessian boots, gleaming black against the skin-tight Wellington trousers, the short regimental skirts of a white marseilles waistcoat. There was something unearthly about the eyes, sunk deeply in their sockets, gaping blankly from the seamed parchment of the face. The hair was snow white, done in a queue at the back of a stiff, high collar. The apparition threw back its head to laugh again. "Yes!" he screamed. "Jean Lafitte! Did you think you could come and take my house like this? You'll all be spitted on my sword."

The wind outside changed direction, whipping in through the door, and the candle was snuffed out, plunging the room into darkness. Denvers staggered back under the impact of a heavy body, felt the hard bite of a ring against his belly as a hand clawed the Le Page from where he had stuck it in his belt. He tried to tear it away, but, when his own hand reached his belt, the Le Page was gone. Then the gun bellowed down by his belly, and he felt the bullet burn across his ribs. He fired blindly ahead of him and then stopped because the girl was calling, and he realized he might hit her.

"Denvers, Denvers, where are you . . . ?"

203

The mad laughter echoed through the high-ceilinged room, and Denvers stumbled across a heavy body. Sheridan? He brought up against the solid mahogany center table, trying to right himself, and another man charged into him. He slugged viciously with the Colt. Six-gun iron clanged off a steel blade, numbing his hand. He sensed the man's thrust, and the blade tore through his shirt as he leaped aside. The cackling laughter rose from in front of him. Ducking another thrust, he tripped over the stairway and stumbled violently backward, having to climb the stairs that way to keep from falling.

"Denvers, is that you on the stairs?"

Again he held his finger on the trigger for fear of hitting Esther and, cursing bitterly, backed on up the stairs.

"Strike your colors!" howled the madman, charging at him.

"Denvers?"

"Esther," he called. "Don't come up the stairs. I'll hit you, if I shoot downwards."

A volley of shots came from down there, and the man in front of Denvers laughed crazily. "You can't kill me. I'm Jean Lafitte."

There was another thunder of shots, and Denvers shouted hoarsely: "Navarra, stop that. Esther's on the stairs."

"The devil with the girl," shouted Navarra from the lower blackness. "Get that madman, Denvers. Get him, I say." He stopped yelling, and there was a scuffle from down there, and Denvers heard the slam of the front door shutting. Then it creaked violently, as if someone had torn it open again, and Navarra's voice sounded muffled by the wind. "Denvers? I thought you were on

204

the stairs . . . ?"

The insane laughter drowned that out, and the man suddenly loomed up on the stairs in front of Denvers, leaping upward with his sword. Denvers lurched forward to meet him, trying to knock the rusty blade aside with his gun. The clang of iron on steel rang through the house again, and Denvers was thrown back, hand numbed as before, barely able to hang onto the Colt. Hot pain seared his shoulder, and he felt the slide of steel through the thick muscles there. With the blade caught in him, Denvers went to his knees on the dancing steps that led to the top landing above him. He hugged his shoulder in to keep the man from pulling the sword out again and turned as he rose, trying to stumble up those last few steps to the level hallway. Jerking desperately at the sword, the man threw himself against Denvers, and they both tripped on the final stair and stumbled across the hall to crash into the opposite wall. A blurred figure rose from behind the newel post and ran past them with a wild shout. Denvers got to his feet again, striking blindly with the gun, rolling down the wall in an effort to free himself from the screaming, clawing madman. He caught the line of light seeping from beneath a door. Then the door was thrust open and that second man who had crouched by the newel post was silhouetted in the lighted rectangle for that moment. "Carnicero?" called Denvers.

"Jean Lafitte," screamed the madman, grasping Denvers's gun wrist with the bestial strength of the demented, finally managing to pull the sword free. Denvers threw himself back from the man's thrust, bounced off the door frame, fell into the lighted room. He flopped over on the floor, tripping up Carnicero as the Mexican tried to jump over him and get out the door. He got one look at the Mexican's dead-white visage. "*Madre de Dios*," screamed Carnicero frenziedly. "*¡La fantasma!*"

"Jean Lafitte," howled the demented creature and lunged at Carnicero.

Carnicero jerked aside, and the sword went through the leg of his flopping white pants, carrying him back against the table, the other man crashing up against him. Denvers shook his head, trying to rise. "See?" he panted. "Carnicero? It's no ghost. Get him, Butcher. He's real, and he's loco, and he'll kill you. Get him!"

Carnicero pulled his long *saca de tripas* out of his belt with a spasmodic jerk, catching the man's sword arm and whirling him around. Now it was the Mexican on the outside, bellied in on the other, holding him against the table. The man gibbered insanely, clawing with dirty, broken nails at Carnicero's face, trying to tear his sword free. Carnicero had the knife back above his head, holding the man by the throat.

"Get him!" shouted Denvers, stumbling to his feet and falling against the wall, pain blinding him. "He's crazy, Butcher. You've got to stop him."

"I can't," bawled the Mexican, still holding his gets-the-guts up in the air. "I never keel a man in my life, Denvers. That's why I couldn't stab you the other day. Not because you save my life on the mainland. I just never keel a man in my life."

"Jean Lafitte," roared the crazy man, tearing his arm loose finally and twisting from between Carnicero and the table. Leaning feebly against the wall, Denvers tried to line up his Colt on the man, but Carnicero's heavy body blocked him off. The Mexican was crying pathetically.

"I can't . . . I can't . . . !"

206

The man caught Carnicero's shirt front in one hand, slamming him around against the table and shifted his feet to lunge. With a last desperate effort Denvers threw himself toward them, gun clubbed, left arm flopping uselessly from his bloody shoulder, but he saw the sword flash up and knew he would be too late. He didn't see exactly what happened then. He saw that Carnicero had dropped his knife arm down to try and ward off the thrust. The two bodies were up against each other for a moment, their feet scuffling on the floor. Carnicero was hidden almost entirely by the other man. There was a last spasmodic reflex. Someone gasped. Denvers stopped himself from falling into them, and the crazy man slipped down against Carnicero, his face turned up in a strange, twisted pain. His arms were around the Mexican, and he slid all the way down, until he was crumpled on the floor with his arms still clasping Carnicero's legs.

"*Dios.*" Carnicero's voice was barely audible, and he glanced dully at the bloody knife in his hand. "It was so easy. I keel him. I didn't think it was like that. Just slipped in so easy. *Dios.* I keel him."

Denvers dropped beside the other man, pulling him off Carnicero's legs, shaking him. "Listen. Who are you? Really. What is all this?"

The man's eyelids fluttered open, and he cackled feebly. "Jean Lafitte. My island. They think Marsala killed me? They think many men killed me. There are a thousand legends. This is the only truth. My island. My Maison Rouge. . . ."

"You killed that Mexican the other night?"

"Aye, and Arno Sheridan," panted the man. "When Sheridan brought his family to this island, he drove me out of the house. Said I had no right to live there. I was

207

just a crazy hermit. I'm not crazy. I'm Jean Lafitte. My house, understand? I caught Sheridan out on the range one day so long ago. He found where I was hiding. I put my sword through him. Just like I put my sword through that Mexican. He was riding herd on the cattle, and he found where I was hiding, too, and I killed him. I'll kill all of you. I'll drive your cattle into the sea and take my house back. . . ."

"It was you cut those cows out the other day?" said Denvers.

Blood frothed the man's lips. "I've been cutting them out for years and driving them over the bluffs above Dagger Point. I had a skiff hidden up there. Somebody took it last night."

"What were you doing on the mainland last night?"

"I go there often. Often. You'd be surprised what I know. A man can hide in the canebrakes and hear many things. I heard Sheriff Giddings and his posse go by. They were talking about that dead horse everybody was hunting. I heard Sinton Navarra and Carnicero go by. They wanted the dead horse, too. I found it before anybody else." He giggled idiotically, coughed up blood. "I was very clever. I took the letter out of the wallet."

The sudden stiffening of Denvers's body caused pain to shoot through his wounded shoulder. "Letter?"

"Yes," laughed the man weakly. "I took it from the wallet, but I left the money in it, and put the wallet back into the *alforjas*, and nobody knew I had taken it, did they? You don't think I'm Lafitte? In my breast pocket. I wrote it. To my brother, Pierre, in Eighteen Twenty-Six. From this very house. How they got hold of it, I don't know, but I wrote it. My letter. You can't have it."

He tried to catch Denvers's hand, but Denvers already

208

had the parchment halfway out of the coat, bloody at one corner. It was then that Esther stumbled in, dropping to her knees beside Denvers. She made a small sound when she saw his wounded shoulder. Then she was looking at the man. "Denvers, who is he?"

"You said it yourself," Denvers told her. "Lot of crazy hermits on this island. Probably got hold of some of those clothes you found in that chest. Navarra?"

Her head rose at that. "Judah ran out the front door, and in the darkness Navarra thought it was you. He went out after Judah. He must have found out his mistake by now."

Her hands slipped off him as he got to his feet, moving toward the door, and his voice was unhurried and deliberate now, because that was the way it stood inside him. "Stay here. I don't want you in the way this time. Stay here till it's over."

## IX

"DENVERS . . . ?"

The hall was dark lower down, but here a candle guttered, suspended in a cast-iron holder, and he went down slowly into increasing shadows with his good shoulder against the wall to conserve his strength.

"That you?" asked Navarra.

Denvers decided he must be at the very foot of the stairs. "It's I. You wanted the letter out of Hardwycke's wallet."

Navarra's voice trembled slightly. "You had it all the time. I'm coming after it."

The creaking started slowly, deliberately, with a small interval between each groan, as a man would make mounting the old stairway unhurriedly. Denvers felt the

209

skin tighten across his sweating face. "You killed Hardwycke for the letter?" he asked.

The noise stopped down there, and for a moment Denvers thought he could hear Navarra's breathing. "Not personally, Denvers. Prieto killed Hardwycke. Prieto and I left New Orleans together, but he stopped off at Refugio while I came on to Matagorda Island. If Prieto missed Hardwycke on the mainland, I'd get him when he arrived here."

"Why should he come here?"

There was a long pause, and Navarra might have been trying to place Denvers exactly during it. Then he spoke. "In New Orleans. Hardwycke had acquired some real estate which originally belonged to the Lafittes, and among the titles he found that the Sheridans had no legal claim on this end of Matagorda. Ostensibly Hardwycke was coming here to force the Sheridans off. However, one of the properties Hardwycke had acquired was the site of the old Lafitte blacksmith shop in New Orleans, and a Negro retainer of Hardwycke's let it leak out that in the floor of the blacksmith shop they had unearthed some old papers of the Lafittes, among them this letter. When I heard that, I knew why Hardwycke had really headed this way. I told you I was an authority on Lafitte. How do you think I became an authority? I've tracked down more of his legendary treasures than any man living and never found a doubloon. But this is the real thing. It's the most gold Lafitte ever had in one spot. I've been hunting that letter half of my life, Denvers.

"You aren't Esther's half-brother?"

"She had a half-brother under the circumstances I told you who died in France," said Navarra. "I was a friend of his, and he left me in charge of his personal effects.

The Sheridans knew of him but had never seen him. When this came up, I took advantage of that. Prieto was my man. Judah hated Caesar Sheridan and feared him, and what man wouldn't have turned against his master for a share in half a million dollars? Carnicero is an old fool, afraid of his own shadow. He was Sheridan's man, but he feared me as much as Sheridan and would do whatever I told him. And now I'm coming, Denvers. I'm coming. . . ."

Denvers saw the sudden shift down there, and Navarra made a shadowy figure behind the curving railing, charging up from the bottom tier of stairs and jumping for the protection of the newel post on that first elliptical landing. He covered his rush with a volley that seemed to shake the house. Denvers ducked down with the lead slapping into the wall behind him, snapping a shot at Navarra, and saw the man throw himself down behind the dancing steps.

"Hold it, Navarra," shouted Denvers. "Let me read you the letter."

"Don't try to stall me, Denvers," called Navarra. "I've come this far, and you won't stop me now. How many shots have you got left in that Colt? Is that what you're doing? You can't bluff me, Denvers."

Denvers spun his cylinder and was surprised to find in the flickering light only one fresh shell. Had he fired that many? He wiped a perspiring palm against his Levi's. "It doesn't matter how many shots a man has, Navarra," he said. "Only how he uses them. Listen to the letter. It's dated June eighteenth, Eighteen Twenty-Six. 'Dear Pierre.' That was Jean's brother?" There was just enough light so that he could make out the ancient script.

"'Dear Pierre,'" he read, holding the letter in his left

211

hand, trembling slightly from the injury to his shoulder, "I am writing you from Matagorda Island, where I have taken abode after I left Galveston. Do not believe any rumors that might reach you of what is happening here. Only what I write in this letter. The men are growing restless, and already one ship's crew has left in the *Pride*. The only one I can trust now is Dominique, and it is with him I shall send this letter. Even Marsala has turned on me. She left the house this morning in a fit of jealous rage and didn't come back until late into the night. Something about a Creole I have been seeing in New Orleans. Which one could that be? There will undoubtedly be talk of a treasure I took when I boarded the *Consolada* last month. It will be false. . . .'"

"Denvers!" Navarra's voice had a hoarse, driven sound. "You're lying. You're making that up to stall for time. There was a treasure, I tell you, and I'm coming. You can't bluff me, Denvers. You can't stop me. Twenty shots, Denvers."

Denvers eared back the hammer with his right thumb. *I'm coming, Denvers. One left against twenty shots*. He went on reading the letter, deliberately, barely able now to make out the old-fashioned script. "'It will be false. Already there has come to my ears a rumor that I have buried treasure here on Matagorda. There is no treasure on the island. . . .'"

"Stop it, Denvers!"

Denvers caught the shift that must have been Navarra, setting himself to rise from his crouching position behind the dancing steps. He grew rigid, the buzzing in his ears louder now, his feet feeling as if they were sinking into a soft, puffy cloud. *Twenty shots*. He remembered that fight on the shore, and what little chance Prieto had stood against that Le Page. *It doesn't matter how many shots a man has, Navarra. Only how he uses them.* Denvers read the last lines of the letter tensely, waiting for Navarra's rush. " 'There is no treasure on the island. The *Consolada* was the only prize I took during my stay here, and she was nothing but a blackbirder off the Gold Coast bound for New Orleans. The few Negroes I took off her didn't bring me enough to buy Marsala a new dress. . . .' "

"Stop it. Damn you!"

Screaming that, Navarra jumped erect on the landing, throwing himself up the last stairs with his gun bucking madly in his hand. Lead whining around him and hitting the back wall in a wild tattoo, Denvers dropped the letter from his left hand and with his right he curled his fingers fully around the Colt's butt. A bullet plucked at his shirt and another clipped his ear. He still couldn't see Navarra very well. The stairway seemed to spin before his eyes. One shot. Navarra shook the whole balcony, coming on up, his gun flaming in his hand. A veritable arsenal. Navarra rounded the turn completely and made a looming target over the Colt's front sight in the flickering light. *It doesn't matter how many shots.* Denvers flexed and winced as a bullet hit him somewhere in his left side. Then his finger pressed the trigger. He heard the boom of the Colt and saw it buck in his hand. Over the sights, Navarra's body stiffened, stumbled up one more step, hovered there, then crashed backward. Denvers swayed forward, dropping the Colt to catch himself before he fell. He was dimly aware of Esther's voice somewhere back of him. Her hands were on him, soft and supporting.

213

## X

THE WIND MADE A FAINT WHINE NOW, FLUTTERING the tails of the three horses as Denvers and Esther and Carnicero headed them up the last dune before the beach. Denvers was still weak from loss of blood, and his shoulder throbbed painfully, but, as long as a hand could fork a horse, he was all right. Esther looked across at him, hair blown over the curve of one flushed cheek. "I can't believe I'm leaving this place. What's it like on the outside, Denvers? Do women really wear satin dresses? My mother used to tell me. And that stuff they use on their hair to make it smell sweet."

"Perfume? You don't need perfume, Esther."

"You'll have to help me, Denvers," she said. "I guess I won't even know how to act."

"You'll know how to act," he said. "And as for helping you, I'll be there as long as you want."

Carnicero giggled. "It's funny, Denvers. All the time I've lived here, and she never looked at me like that."

The girl flushed and then, to hide her confusion, looked back toward the old house. "I guess it was best, that crazy man dying there. I don't see how an old man like that could be so strong. He must have been past eighty." She shivered suddenly, eyes darkening as she turned to Denvers. "Who do you think he was, Denvers, really?"

"Jean Lafitte," Denvers said, and there was only wonder in his eyes as he added, "or maybe just his ghost."

214

# ABOUT THE AUTHOR

LES SAVAGE, JR. was an extremely gifted writer, born in Alhambra, California, but he grew up in Los Angeles. His first published story was "Bullets and Bullwhips" accepted by the prestigious Street & Smith's *Western Story*. Almost ninety more magazine stories, all set on the American frontier, followed, many of them published in Fiction House magazines such as *Frontier Stories* and *Lariat Story Magazine* where Savage became a superstar with his name on many covers. His first novel, **Treasure of the Brasada**, appeared in 1947, the first of twenty-four published novels to appear in the next decade. Due to his preference for historical accuracy, Savage often ran into problems with book editors in the 1950s who were concerned about marriages between his protagonists and women of different races—a commonplace on the real frontier but not in much Western fiction in that decade. As a result of the censorship imposed on many of his works, only now have they been fully restored by returning to the author's original manuscripts.

Much as Stephen Crane before him, while he wrote the shadow of his imminent death grew longer and longer across his young life, and he knew that, if he was going to do it at all, he would have to do it quickly. He did it well, better than almost anyone who wrote Western and frontier fiction, ever. Now that his novels and stories are being restored to what he had intended them to be, his achievement irradiated by his powerful and profoundly sensitive imagination will be with us always, as he had wanted it to be, as he had so rushed

215

against time and mortality that it might be. Among his most recent publications are *Fire Dance At Spider Rock* (Five Star Westerns, 1995), *Medicine Wheel* (Five Star Westerns, 1996), *Copper Bluffs* (Circle Ⓥ Westerns, 1996), *The Legend of Señorita Scorpion* (Circle Ⓥ Westerns, 1996), *Coffin Gap* (Five Star Westerns, 1997), *The Return of Señorita Scorpion: A Western Trio* (Circle Ⓥ Westerns, 1997), and *Phantoms in the Night* (Five Star Westerns, 1998). *The Shadow in Renegade Cañon: A Western Trio* will be his next Circle Ⓥ Western, containing another short novel in the *Señorita* Scorpion saga.